# DADDY'S BOY

# DADDY'S BOY

SHANDANA MINHAS

First published in hardback in India in 2016 by Fourth Estate
An imprint of HarperCollins *Publishers* India

Building 10, Tower A, 4th Floor, DLF Cyber City, Phase II,
Gurugram Haryana – 122002, India
www.harpercollins.co.in



P-ISBN: 978-93-5177-714-4
E-ISBN: 978-93-5177-715-1

2 4 6 8 10 9 7 5 3 1



Typeset in 11/15 Sabon LT Std by
R. Ajith Kumar

Printed and bound at
MicroPrints India, New Delhi

*For IY*

*Hatred seems to open the same glands as love:*
*it even produces the same actions.*

Graham Greene

# PROLOGUE

# PAKISTAN STANDARD

YOUR RIGHT TO KNOW

Established Daily • April 28, 2013 • Jumada t-Tania 17, 1434 AH

## Carnage in Karachi: 5 killed, 40 injured

*Staff Reporter*

KARACHI: Anti-state elements continued their assault on the upcoming democratic transition of power as two major parties came under attack on the campaign trail in three different bombings in Karachi on Saturday. The attacks killed 5 people and injured more than 40.

Two different blasts near the Muttahida Qaumi Movement (MQM) election office in Orangi Town, one in Qasba Colony and one outside a Shia imambargah, claimed two lives and 25 casualties.

Pakistan Peoples Party (PPP) candidate for PS-111 was injured in another blast in Lyari, along with 19 others. Three people, including a woman, were killed.

The explosions were heard even from far away and damaged all nearby buildings and vehicles. The resultant power blackout spread further fear amongst citizens and led to delay in shifting of dead and injured to nearby hospitals.

Saturday's attacks make a total of five terrorist attacks in the city in as many days, in which 26 have died. No group has so far claimed responsibility for the Saturday attacks but the banned Tehrik-i-Taliban Pakistan (TTP) had declared to target all secular political parties in the country and previously claimed responsibility for the Thursday and Friday attacks on the Awami National Party (ANP) and MQM.

The MQM has announced a day of mourning throughout Sindh on Sunday. It has appealed to masses to keep businesses and transport shut today.

The surge of violence in the financial hub of the nation has increased concerns about law and order in the run up to the general elections on 11 May. An anonymous, highly-placed sourced in the PPP told this reporter, 'Free and fair elections? You tell me, is it fair that when we say we are dying to vote, we have to mean it literally?'

# ONE

IT WAS THAT RAREST of Karachi deaths. Expected.

The pavements baked in the April heat but a slow drizzle began as ICU staff removed tubes from Anis Nabi's collapsed veins. A nurse unscrewed the catheter and wiped away the blood pooled in the creases of his neck. Another passed one hand lightly over his forehead, then pulled the sheet up to cover his face. Wheeling his body down to the morgue – the access corridor lined with empty stretchers, no one in sight but a flirting couple that disappeared at the first prospect of discovery – the orderlies heard the freak shower gather momentum and cursed, anticipating a risky journey home through standing water and the threat of arbitrary electrocution as the city's decrepit power distribution system collapsed. But by evening, as his body lay in the hospital till the cheque cleared and it could be released, the clouds had moved on.

Miles away, they massed over the wind-beaten, dilapidated suburb where the patriarch had lived. A torrential downpour descended; drops the size of pebbles beat on the windows of his fourth-floor flat, demanding to be let in.

The three old men, slouched around a dimly lit card table in what used to be the patriarch's living room, approved.

'He would have appreciated this,' said one.

'He would have said the heavens themselves weep at my passing or something equally dramatic,' said another.

'No,' said the third, 'he would have said, well, I died with a full bladder and I had to take a leak somewhere.'

Their chuckles and chortles, sniggers and howls, drowned out the sound of the key turning in the lock. A young man in a pink shirt and dark suit with thick black hair gelled off his forehead had entered and now stood by the door, waiting to be invited further in. A small grey suitcase rested equally primly by his side. But the old men around their table did not notice him till he cleared his throat, politely, during a lull in the laughter. He met their eyes, pointedly not looking down at the bottles or glasses on the table between them.

'Salam alaikum,' the visitor said, 'I'm...'

'It's a ghost!'

'Trust him to come back forty years younger!'

'You must be Asfandyar,' the third rose and urged the youth forward with an outstretched hand, lurching only slightly as he shook it, placing his other hand on Asfandyar's face and leaning into him to steady himself. 'My god, you look exactly like your father...'

'I'll take your word for it.'

'Don't take something that means nothing to him, you fool, take his watch!'

The fat man who had drawn the visitor in dissolved into giggles that rose to a crescendo, accompanied by the similar merriment it inspired in his companions.

Asfandyar, thinking their drinking, their mirth, indecorous in a dead man's home, felt embarrassed for them and looked around the room. The windows were closed and must have been for a while; the air smelt stale and musty. A thin cover of dust lay on every visible surface. There was an alcove kitchen to the right, with no visible evidence of food production or consumption, just a half-empty bag of ice cubes lying dazed on a counter, a few spilling out, like animals had been at it. To the left, with its back against a view of the still waters the taxi driver had told him was Boat Basin, lay a well-worn brown velvet two-seater with a coffee table on one side and tall bookshelves on the other. There was an indentation on the left of the sofa, the fabric was shiny, the seat depressed. *That must be*, he thought, *where my father used to sit and read*. He had never pictured his father as a reading man. He had tried not to picture him at all. He turned his face away from the door that lay open on the other side of the card table that dominated the room – a glimpse of the foot of a bed was to him an as yet unearned intimacy – and back towards the company. He must have taken a minute to look around, because they had fallen silent. Above the scrawny wrists and withered necks visible through their voluminous kurtas, three sets of inquiring eyes contemplated him with an intensity that made him even more uncomfortable than their inappropriate glee.

'I'm Asfandyar Ikram,' he said. 'I was told you would be expecting me.'

'And we're Iftikhar, Shaukat and Gulzar.'

'Or Ifty, Shaukoo and Gullo, if you'd like to know what your father called us, apart from his brothers.'

'Guess which one is which correctly and you win your first drink!'

'I don't drink.' He hadn't meant to say it as loudly as he did. But he was wondering if he had accidentally let himself into the wrong place.

'More for us then! That should teach Ifty some manners. Offering a man a drink before telling him he's sorry his father died. I'm Gulzar. Gulzar Uncle. I've been waiting to meet you again for a long, long time. I'm sorry it has to be under these circumstances,' the fat one who had breathed alcohol into his face told him. 'You can call me Gullo too, if you like.'

'Why should I tell him I'm sorry his father died? I didn't kill Anis.' The tall one whose cheekbones protruded like polished knobs from a gaunt face spoke. 'I'm Iftikhar. Your father was my brother. So you can call me Ifty Uncle.'

'I'm Shaukat.' Shaukat was the shortest, his skull a third eye in the light of the lamp in the corner. 'I'm sorry for your loss. And mine. And don't call me unless it's an emergency.'

Asfandyar found himself wanting to smile. His mother had warned him about 'the patriarch's handmaidens'. *Don't get too familiar*, she had said. *With those three it'll breed affection*. And nothing else, beyond *they'll tell you what you need to do*. 'I'm Asfandyar Ikram,' he repeated instead.

'Asfandyar Ikram, huh? Well, Asfandyar Ikram, we

haven't seen you since you were Asfandyar Nabi, waddling around, shitting all over the place till your mother badgered your father into putting diapers on you.'

'Anis wanted to raise you like God made you, naked.'

'Crying.'

'Shitting. Don't forget shitting.'

'God doesn't make us shitting, you idiot, that happens later, when we try to eat the world.'

'Fair point. But your mother disagreed.'

'Haan. Jehanara was a real stickler for disagreement.'

'Had a natural talent for it, if I remember correctly.'

'How is your mother anyway? We haven't seen her for as long as your father hasn't.'

'Hadn't.'

'Nazi.'

'She's fine.' He felt he might have made her sound callous. Which she wasn't. Any more than she was a 'stickler for disagreement'. She was a peacemaker, a negotiator, a healer. 'Well, when I say fine I mean…'

'We know what you mean.'

'We know your mother.'

How could they? When they hadn't met her as long as his father. 'She said one of you would meet me at the airport.'

'And an optimist. Did I mention she was an optimist too?'

'Only an optimist would have married Anis.'

'But then there's the pragmatism of her having left him…'

'Noted. An optimistic pragmatic... '

'Who thinks grown men need rides from airports.'

'When everyone knows a taxi and the keys left with the chowkidar will do.'

'Unless she knows something about the grown man that we don't.'

'He has a condition, perhaps?'

'An unusual fear of taxis?'

'Taxophobia!'

'No. Taxophobia is what you have, an unusual fear of taxes. This would be taxiphobia.'

'It can't be genetic, in this case.'

'Early childhood trauma?'

'A taxi drive gone wrong?'

'An unforeseen destination?'

'Start out for the zoo and find yourself bent over a table at the doctor's, perhaps?'

'Is that what happened?'

'Did the bad doctor hurt little Asfandyar?'

'Awful place, Lahore.'

'Savage. Rampaging bands of doctors.'

'Weren't there mobs of them running riot through the streets in your city last year, shrieking for higher salaries while their patients died unattended?'

'Actually, nobody died.' Asfandyar, battling the guilt of letting people he didn't know criticize his mother, felt he should at least defend his city. And its doctors. Karachiites were famed for their antipathy to Lahore, a friend had warned him, and he should stand firm against their prejudice. They were jealous of its peace, its culture, its architecture, its metro bus system and its motorway. Karachi had no motorway. It had underpasses and flyovers. And the buses didn't have sliding doors; they had no doors at all.

'Your father didn't approve of doctors either, you know,' Gullo confided.

'Or Lahore.'

'Hated them with a passion. It's why he died at home, alone.'

'Technically, with a cute nurse by his side.'

'Maintaining a respectable distance.'

'Easy to do considering the size of his bed. Why did he have such a big bed anyway?'

'I don't know,' Shaukat paused to consider, rubbing his scalp with one hand as he thought. 'He seemed to like it though. He certainly spent a lot of time in it towards the end. I hope they lock the door in the morgue so his body doesn't walk out and try to come back to it.'

'But he didn't spend a lot of time in bed with the cute nurse,' Ifty said to Asfandyar, 'if that's what you were thinking.'

'I wasn't thinking…'

'Excellent! A complete absence of thought!' Shaukat whacked his hand hard enough on the table for the glasses to jump. 'That's a sign of good health in a young man!'

'I'm thirty years old,' Asfandyar felt obliged to point out, feeling a little like he had felt when he had taken his mother to meet his fiancée's parents.

'So you are, Asfandyar Ikram, so you are.'

'Thank you for reminding us how old we are,' Ifty raised a hand to his forehead in mock horror. 'I feel ancient suddenly.'

'Like you should just crawl into a hole and die? Me too.' Gullo nodded sagely. 'Me too.'

'I'm not dying in any hole. Certainly not this one.' They had a rhythm, Asfandyar noted, as Shaukat cut in; everybody took turns. Where had his father fit in? 'I'm going to die in a bed. A nice, comfortable bed. In my sleep.'

'With a cute nurse by your side?'

'I'll have you know I'm a married man, Ifty, and only I am allowed to refer to my wife that way.'

'If I was talking about your wife, I wouldn't have said cute, would I?'

'Shaukoo...'

'Gullo?'

'Darling!' said Ifty querulously, as if hurt to be excluded.

'I think you should give Asfandyar a chair.'

'Why? Is it his birthday?'

'No. I think he's about to fall over.'

Indeed, the son of the patriarch swayed gently on his feet. A weakness swept over him. Last night, in Lahore, he had fallen asleep to the pleasant sound of his fiancée on the phone. The next morning, he had woken to his mother – who hardly ever came into his room – shaking his shoulder and telling him a father he hadn't even known was alive was dead. Then he was told he needed to fly to Karachi and bury him and do what was needed for him to collect his inheritance. *What do you mean bury my father? Did somebody dig him up?* He hadn't even known he had an inheritance! His mother had promised to answer all his questions *when you come back, not now, I have a lot to do and so do you*, and told him he would be met at the airport by old friends of his father's who were the closest thing the man had had to a family. Sitting in Lahore's airport lounge for the two hours his flight was delayed, he had decided to think about what was safest and spent most of it wondering what the old friends would be like. They would probably, he had thought, be men made toothless by good intentions, like the uncles one saw at weddings, standing patiently in the corner, talking about cricket and the military, till a wife crooked a finger and one scuttled forward to attend to her. Or they would be stoic beards rendered silent by the mortality of repeated funerals. They would treat him with the respect accorded to the recently bereaved. He would reciprocate. They might be standoffish, depending on what their relationship with his mother had been in the years about which he knew nothing. He would maintain a studied emotional distance at all times.

He had stepped out of the arrivals exit with what he considered a suitable mien, willing passivity to his features and strength to his eyes, but none of the men in the crush outside would catch his eye, and a young woman his gaze had passed over twice had marched up to him and asked him, waspishly, in Urdu, what the hell he was looking at. Who left people stranded at airports in the most dangerous city in the world? Rude, inconsiderate, immature, incorrigible drunks!

He had loitered like a fool in the arrivals area for an hour, beating off increasingly aggressive touts promising him everything from 'best hotel' to 'best rate for anything, sir', before going to the white cab booth and hiring one to take him to the address his mother had given him, *as a precaution.* The taxi driver had spent the entire ride telling him how bad things were in the city. What to do should a mob stop them? Jump out and run. How hard he had worked to get his Master's degree only to end up driving a cab. Rich people *lived*, poor people *existed*. They had driven through frantic traffic into what seemed to be a freak thunderstorm. Lightning fractured the sky. In between, there were volleys of gunshots. Then it had taken them an extra fifteen minutes to find the right commercial building, tucked into a small lane close to Shireen Jinnah Colony, which, Asfandyar learnt from the garrulous driver, was one of Karachi's many gateways to hell. Another five minutes to convince the brusque chowkidar to slide back the iron gate and let Asfandyar into the foyer and another minute being told off for addressing him in Punjabi and learning from him that Punjabis did not rule the world before he threw across a set of keys and turned back to the Election 2013 coverage he was watching.

He went into the wrong elevator, not noticing the 'Brokan' sign on it till he emerged. He had been stuck in it for fifteen minutes pounding helplessly at the door, battling claustrophobia. Eventually, two children with crowbars had pried it open from the outside, chattering happily to each other in what he thought was Sindhi as they worked, then laughed at him and ran away after snatching the hundred rupee note he offered.

The shock of the many little humiliations he had endured that day, coupled with the vague feeling he was getting deeper into an environment he couldn't control, threatened to overwhelm Asfandyar. He had had several panic attacks as a teenager and his mother had taught him to conquer them. He took deep breaths and placed a hand on the table and commanded his thoughts to form an orderly queue. He reminded himself of the routine that was his life. He went to bed at the same time. He woke up at the same time. He had worked at the same office as a human resource manager since he had done his MBA. He had a fiancée called Lalarukh whom he saw twice a week for dinner and spoke to every night before going to sleep. He lived with his mother in a pleasant, old house where the electricity went for only four hours a day and everybody used two words when they could use seven. That was his life. It was a quiet life. Everything went according to plan. That would continue to be his life. This was just something that was happening. It was here. He was in it. It would pass. He would still be who he was. He was a strong, capable man, and he would handle it. His legs were shaking because he hadn't eaten since afternoon. That was all. He tried to stop shaking but the weakness worsened the more his body fought it.

'Is he all right?'

'Of course he's all right, he just hasn't got his sea legs yet.'

'If he's as much his father's son as he looks, he will. Here,' Asfandyar felt a chair nudge the back of his knees and slipped gratefully onto it, 'have a seat. Have a drink.'

'I don't drink.'

'It's the good stuff.'

'No, thank you.'

'Are you sure?'

'Shaukoo, you bastard, leave the boy alone, can't you see he's hungry?'

'Where did you put the kababs?'

'In the microwave.'

As Shaukoo bustled about the alcove kitchen, taking plates out of cabinets and assembling a tray – Asfandyar noted the ease of practice – Ifty and Gullo peppered him with questions. Had he had an uneventful flight? Were the new airhostesses as attractive as the old ones used to be? Why the hell did they have to call them flight attendants now? Didn't Asfandyar think all the male ones were homosexual? No? Did Asfandyar perhaps have a problem with homosexuality? Did he also think that now that the supreme court has declared there needed to be a third column for the transgendered, there would soon be a fourth column for gay people? Were there any gay people in Lahore apart from the chief minister?

'My wife sent these for you.' Shaukoo slammed the tray onto the centre of the table, plates stacked roughly on the side of a platter of kababs and another of paratha, and barked 'Eat!' before Asfandyar could thank him. He wrestled with how to phrase his gratitude. *That was very kind of her. Please thank aunty for me?* But he was afraid of the response it might engender. *Who're you calling aunty! No one's ever accused my wife of kindness. And survived.* He realized he was afraid of anything they said. There was an urchin-like quality to them. Give them an inch and they might take your car. He let it pass. The men set to.

Asfandyar felt that men eating together was the one place where there was solidarity among strangers. Eating was like congregational praying. Everyone knew the rules and, in all-male gatherings, without the interference of the petty observations of women or the feigned manners of their presence, everyone respected them. Elbows didn't matter. Food was sacrosanct.

The kababs were excellent. Fresh meat, with just the right balance of mint and chilli, they melted in his mouth. Lahore's Gawalmandi, he felt, would have been hard-pressed to offer any better.

'Please thank aunty for me. Please tell her they were excellent,' Asfandyar said, emboldened by the meal.

'I would, if she'd actually made them.'

'He wishes his wife could cook like this.'

'He wishes his wife would do a lot of things.'

'Remember what Anis used to tell you? If your woman gets angry, you have to get angrier. Let her ride you once and you'll spend the rest of your life on your hands and knees.'

'You would know.'

'Why? Have you been watching us through the window?'

'Where can I wash up?' Asfandyar asked desperately.

'That depends on what you want to wash.'

'My hands.'

'Stop being so immature, Ifty, the young man has no interest in your toilet humour. He's only interested in the toilet.'

'Anywhere. It's your house.'

'No, it isn't.' He said that more loudly than he had intended to, as well.

'It will be.'

'My mother said…'

'We can talk about that tomorrow, no need to burden you with details tonight.'

Asfandyar chose the room on thc right, the one that didn't have a bed in it. Three-fourths of it were obscured by a tarp covering what seemed to be a mess of clutter. Chair legs, more books, a child's guitar peeking out from under a corner.

The bathroom was small. Pink. A razor balanced on one edge of the sink, a soap dish with a sliver of Dettol rested on the other. When he got back to the table he found the tray and the dishes had already been cleared up, stacked on a counter. He would strike early in this round, he resolved as he took his seat, and set the agenda.

'My mother said my father had left instructions for you to give me.'

'We'll talk about them tomorrow.'

'If they're in printed form, perhaps you could just let me have copies and I'll look over them.'

'You can. In the morning.'

'If there is someone else I can talk to, just so I have a better idea of what to expect tomorrow...'

'Why would you want to talk to anyone else?'

'You just got here, and already you're underestimating the pleasure of our company.'

'The last person who did that ended up dead.'

*Was that a threat?* They all stared at him impassively.

'Relax! I'm talking about your father!'

Asfandyar's eyes widened. He considered his chances. The three were elderly and inebriated. He could shove the table over and make it to the door. What if they caught him in the stairwell? The bald one's fingers were tapered and cruel.

'Shaukoo doesn't mean we killed him, Asfandyar, he means your father was always complaining about our inability to conduct civilized discourse,' Gullo said.

Was his face so transparent? Lalarukh had always said she couldn't tell what he was thinking, it was so difficult to read.

'He died a natural death, then?' He had meant it as a genuine question, but still he cringed. This wasn't how death and its aftermath were supposed to unfurl. What had his mother sent him into? It was best to leave, and try it again in the light of day. 'I should go, then, and meet you in the morning so we can...'

'We'll talk about all the details in the morning.'

'It's just, I was asking because I need to schedule my day...'

'Why? Will it be your last one on earth?'

'Hopefully not, but I like to be prepared.'

'How can you prepare to put someone you love into the ground?'

'I didn't...' he trailed off.

'You didn't love your father?'

'My father didn't love me either.' He heard a child's petulance in his voice. Both his mother and his fiancée would have said it was out of character for him. Perhaps he was still sitting in Lahore airport's departure lounge? He had fallen asleep. This was a dream.

'You don't know that.'

'I don't know that because I didn't know him.' Now irritation. His skin seemed translucent.

He was clearly hallucinating, he told himself. He could see the veins in his own hand throbbing. The hyenas had no business raking it up. In a dream, he could tell them that. So he told them that.

'You hyenas have no business raking this up.'

'Oh no, we offended the little Nabi!'

'Why you didn't know your father is something that only your mother can explain to you. It wouldn't be appropriate for us to comment.'

'Appropriate? Appropriate!' Asfandyar threw his head back and laughed.

'Young man, it might not seem so to you, but we're mourning.'

'The way your father wanted us to.'

'Tomorrow, we'll mourn the other way. Tonight, we mourn the way Anis would have.'

'Right.' He felt hostility. The fingers had curled a little tighter around the glasses. The eyes were directed at the tabletop. His status as an outsider was communicated to him. He felt a sense of isolation so suffocating, the claustrophobia of the elevator came back to him. That's when he knew it wasn't a dream. A memory in a dream would not be this intense. The rain still beat at the windows and a chill had crept in. 'Could any of you recommend a good guesthouse?'

'We can.' Gullo looked at the others, as if for confirmation, before continuing. 'If you have a drink with us before you go.'

'I don't drink.'

'When you say you don't drink, do you mean you've never had a drink or that you don't want to have a drink?'

'I don't want to have a drink.' He had read a news item on the plane that Pakistan's foremost brewery – there were only three – had paid a record Rs 314 million in taxes from sales in the first four months of this year alone. He felt he was in the company of people who contributed significantly to that amount and did not feel, that day, like he wanted to add to it.

'We're not sharab kay tablighi, you know,' Gullo said gently.

'Speak for yourself.' Shaukoo feigned indignation.

'Anis left this fine beverage on his bedside table. Unopened. With a ribbon around it,' Ifty told Asfandyar.

'Liar,' Shaukoo threw that over his shoulder as he headed for the ice cubes still melting on the counter.

'Fine. There was no ribbon. There was a note though. For my son. Drink it with him so that he knows who I was.'

'— An old drunkard with not much to show for his life except a bunch of good for nothing friends,' Gullo added.

'And a cute nurse.'

'Was that in the note?'

'Fine, that wasn't in the note.'

'But the bit about drink it with him so that he knows who I was, that's true. See for yourself.' Ifty turned the bottle around so Asfandyar could see it. There was a note taped to the side of it. *For my son. Drink it with him so that he knows who I was.* It was printed in block letters, in fountain pen.

'I don't drink.' But his protestation was weaker. *For my son* ... had his father written that? Had he been thinking of him, before he died? Had he thought of him at all in the decades between them? His stomach was lined now. And he wasn't averse to the occasional beer, when he could be confident that his mother or his fiancée would not know about it. How different could whiskey be?

'Until this morning, neither did we.'

'Really?'

'Really. Like your father used to say, every day is a fresh start, the slate wiped clean.'

'And if every day doesn't feel like a fresh start, get back in bed and stay there till it does.'

'How do you know I'm not going to call the police and tell them there are people in this apartment breaking the law?'

It took five minutes for the laughter to die down. 'Son,' Ifty managed to say finally, once he'd patted Shaukoo on the back till he stopped choking, 'there have been four bomb blasts in Karachi in the last forty-eight hours. You know what the police are going to say if you call them and say there are three old men drinking peacefully in an apartment? Well, don't just sit there, join them!'

'If your father was here, instead of being dead,' Gulloo added, 'he would have told you that the story of Karachi is the story of alcohol. Once upon a time, you could drink in peace as long as you didn't break the peace. Now you have to drink in secret so you can find peace. And he would have told you that the story of alcohol in Karachi is the story of bootleggers. First, there was only one bootlegger that everybody seemed to use. His name was Ramesh. One day people compared notes on how he managed to do seven different deliveries simultaneously. Then they realized it was several different people who all used the name Ramesh because Muslims were more comfortable buying from somebody they thought was non-Muslim. After that, it was a string of khaalis Urdu-speaking uncles who had compact cars and impeccable manners because the Muslims had realized how much money there was in it. And now it's burger kids in four-wheel drives who went to good schools. They bring a servant to carry bottles from car to car.' He laughed. 'Your father found that hysterical. He said new money always went straight to old habits.'

'I'm assuming my father wasn't a religious man.'

That only set them off again. This time, Shaukoo answered. 'Oh, he was. He was a deeply religious man. He was so religious,' he took a moment to have another fit of giggling, 'he was so deeply religious he went right through it and came out on the other side!'

'Did he pray?'

'All the time. If you believe, like he did, that these days living itself is an act of faith.'

'Did he fast?'

'Well, I can assure you, he certainly never slowed.'

'Where will he be buried?'

'In the naval graveyard off national stadium. Next to your dada, dadi.'

'When did they die?' He knew he would be hurt if they had been alive too and he hadn't known them.

'Before you were born. In a shipwreck. When we were all cadets. He'd taken your mother to the cinema.'

'We were waiting outside to tell him when they came out.'

'Your mother hit Gullo with her handbag for making him cry in public.'

'I didn't know he was in the navy.'

'He wasn't. We were in the merchant navy.'

'Your grandfather was in the other navy.'

'It seems you don't know a lot of things you should have known.'

'Tell me.'

'Have a drink with us, and we'll tell you.'

Jehanara Ikram would be disappointed if her son capitulated. But her son was disappointed that his mother had hidden things he had a right to know. He had grown up thinking his mother had been widowed, young, by a husband she couldn't stand to be reminded of. As a child, when he asked her about his father, she would burst into tears. So he stopped asking. He grew used to filling in the details from his imagination. They would vary according to his reading, his mood. One day, his father had been a pilot in the war. The next, he had been a feudal lord. Once, he had been a married man who had ruined her. The details changed. But he would note the men of their acquaintance, her cousins and colleagues that she said positive things about. He would be searching for clues in their demeanour to the qualities of the man she had once been married to. Women married men they admired, didn't they? Surely what she liked in the men she knew was what she had liked in his father. Patience. Kindness. Stoicism. A good head for numbers. At some point in his adolescence, young Asfandyar had marched up to his mother and declared triumphantly that he knew his father had been an accountant. Jehanara had kissed him, thrice, once on each eye and once on the forehead, and told him he was a sweetie pie. When he'd asked about his dada, dadi, she told him his father was raised in an orphanage. The truth, he now knew, was that his father had been some sailorman with whiskey for blood, his dada, dadi had been lost at sea, and she herself had been the sort of woman who hit people with handbags on the street.

'To Anis.' Ifty raised his glass.

'To Anis!'

'To Anis!'

'To my father.' So Asfandyar Ikram, previously Asfandyar Nabi, raised a drink to his lips. He knew he shouldn't. He knew it was a sin. He knew his fiancée would not approve, and that his mother would not either, but the eyes of the old men around the table at that moment were as kind and brimming with emotion as they had been since he entered. The second he raised his glass, in place of weakness or hostility, he felt warmth emanating from his surroundings, and felt if he took a sip, he too would be enveloped in it. After he took another, they poured some ice water into his whiskey. And two sips turned into three. And then four. And then the glass was empty and needed to be refilled. And the bottle had no bottom. And the Jewish woman Anis had once met in a bar in Hong Kong did. And the woman in Bombay was jealous. And he'd had to borrow bail money from the ship's captain when she swung a punch and Shaukoo stepped in-between. And smuggle cigarettes to repay it. And Dhaka wasn't what it used to be. And Karachi wasn't either. And none of them had ever understood why the new women in the new malls dressed like prostitutes but acted like nuns. And there was the time they had to rush that nun to the hospital in Singapore and the doctor had asked which one of them was her husband and Anis had felt duty-bound to avenge her honour by slapping him. Anis had loved women. Women had loved Anis. Anis had a temper. Anis was kind. Anis could speak four languages fluently and order in seven. Anis had been admired. Anis had been reviled. Anis had been bereft. The evening passed, as such evenings do, with all other senses being subservient to sound. The sound of conversation. The sound of storytelling. In that evening's stories, the son met the father.

There were stories of the present too. Asfandyar told them about his job. It was a good job, with prospects for advancement in the near future, if he played his cards right. He told them about his fiancée, Lalarukh, and how they had met in college. Her best friend had been in love with him, so they had waited till she got married before they got together, to protect her feelings. Gullo and Ifty thought that was sweet. Shaukoo said it meant he didn't particularly like Lalarukh, and Anis would have told him that too. Asfandyar insisted he more than liked her. Shaukoo challenged him to name three things about her he liked that didn't fit into a boy's sketch of female anatomy. Asfandyar called her and told her a joke and put her on speakerphone so they could hear her laughter, then panicked and hung up. He agonized over whether she had noticed he was drunk. Gullo and Ifty assured him she would only think he had been understandably overwhelmed. Shaukoo told him it only confirmed his theory that there was little but a fear of the alternative between them. Asfandyar was too drunk to remember he hadn't told her why he was in Karachi. He began hyperventilating, and they distracted him with stories about Anis. The time Anis stole a particularly harsh instructor's pet chicken and persuaded the mess cook to serve it to him for dinner. The time Anis fell overboard and swam for fourteen hours to survive. The time a PTI volunteer came to the door to tell him about Imran Khan's vision and Anis said *young man, you want to talk to me about love, I'm listening. You want to talk to me about politics, go fuck yourself.* The time a neighbour came to the door asking him if he prayed and Anis told him, *Do I pray? Of course I pray! Just this morning I prayed that Allah send me a nosy neighbor asking intrusive personal questions so I can hit him in the head with my cricket bat and here you are! Allah be praised!* Asfandyar laughed so hard he cried. His father had been a brave man, a funny man, a thief. His mother called him too, and the trio sat with straight faces in perfect silence as he told her, with an equally straight face, that yes he had been picked up, that yes matters of inheritance and logistics had been discussed, no it was not terribly strange for him to be where he was. He was a man. The strange, strangers, the peculiar, they were his element. Why had she never taught him that? Why had she never told him about his father? Why did she think he was tired and should go to bed?

Later, the old men who had been his father's sidekicks steered him gently into the bedroom. They did not seem as drunk as they had when he had entered. If anything, they seemed sober.

'You toleme it was huge!' Asfandyar protested, as he rolled onto the single bed and turned and almost rolled off the other side.

'We lied.'

'You lie a lot!'

'We do.'

'Shouldn lie. Lyin bad.'

'Spoken like a true Nabi.'

'Did he really die in it?'

'No. He died in the hospital.'

'Was he alone?'

'We were all with him.'

'We took a stereo and played his favorite ghazal. *Main kapray badal kar jaoon kahan, aur baal banaoon kis kay liyay...*'

'Gullo here pretended to be a cute nurse.'

'He died laughing.'

They waited till he had fallen asleep before leaving. One stayed behind, curled up on the charpoy pulled out from beneath the tarp in the next room where the cook used to sleep when the patriarch had been healthy enough to still have an appetite, in case his son woke in the night needing comfort. Outside, the rain had stopped beating against the windows. It now licked them, gently, like a dog licking the cheeks of its dead master, asking him to rise again.

# TWO

ASFANDYAR WOKE TO THE sound of a struggle. Two pigeons fought on a windowsill as light flooded through grimy glass. He watched with one eye as a bird rose briefly into the air to deliver a kick to the other's plumage. The other eye remained shut, lost in the soft depths of the feather pillow his head rested on. A fan beat a dance-like rhythm to avian movements. He wondered idly whose pigeons they were. In Lahore, people kept them as pets on rooftops, marking their ownership with coloured bands around the birds' legs. These birds weren't wearing any bands. As the bout escalated into a full-fledged brawl, feathers flying, beaks engaging, the cooing increasing in volume and tone till it seemed the fighters had moved beyond questions of ancestry to questions of existence itself, Asfandyar realized he was in Karachi. *I'm in the bed my father died in.* Trying not to move his hands or touch any more of it than he absolutely had to, he looked around for evidence of blood, or fluids, sniffed the pillow his head had been on, but beyond a faint whiff of oil, smelt nothing. Perhaps the nurse had covered the mattress with a plastic sheet. He had no recollection of how he had come to sleep on it. He sat up and peeled back the blanket draped over his legs.

The room was furnished with a side table with a utilitarian reading lamp on it and one old wingback chair.

His belt lay coiled on the seat. His suit jacket hung neatly on a hanger on the hook on the back of the half-open door. A card table, devoid of glasses, bottles or dust, was visible through it. *How did I get here?* There was a horrible taste in his mouth. The wicker blind had been pulled all the way up to let the day into the room. The harsh sunlight hurt his eyes. Across the pigeons, a few feet, he could see directly into the bedroom of a flat in an adjacent building. A man sat cross-legged on a sofa in a banyaan, scratching his armpit as he watched TV. *Water*, he thought.

Someone had taken his shoes and socks off and slid them under the bed. When he bent to reach for them, a rush of blood to the head drove him upright immediately. *Water.* A plastic jug and glass rested on the side table. He drained it. He stood barefoot in the door to the bathroom for a full minute, staring in horrified fascination at the geometric black and white patterns on the tiles. *This is an optical illusion,* his brain told him, *you must keep looking at it till you see a face.*

He splashed cold water on his face till his skin tingled. In the mirror, bloodshot eyes stared back at him under a furrowed forehead and a cockatoo tuft where the hair that hadn't been enveloped in a pillow had won its freedom. There was only one toothbrush, and a toothpaste for sensitive gums. He couldn't use it. *What am I going to catch, my father's genes? My father's germs. I don't want them.* He opened the cabinet behind the mirror, found a bottle of Listerine, and gargled. Someone seemed to have placed a bowl over his head, or he was underwater, the sound reached him in distorted waves. He spat. He stared at himself in the mirror. Suspiciously. He felt his body wasn't his own, that he was merely driving it. Another face looked at his in the mirror, over his shoulder, suspiciously. Chubby, jet-eyed, brow furrowed.

Gullo leaned against the doorjamb, raised one arm over his head, placed the other hand where his waist would have been had he one and cooed, 'Last night was wonderful, jani. You were so strong. So tender...'

Asfandyar closed the door gently, put the lid of the commode down and sat on it. The pattern had faces and they swam in and out of focus. Uncles danced gaily across the tiles. Gullo. Ifty. Shaukoo. He rose, flushed, washed his hands and opened the door again. The room was empty. But his suitcase waited by his bed, a clean towel folded across the top of it. Cutlery banged about outside, and he saw plates set on the card table.

Gullo perused an Urdu newspaper and sipped a cup of black coffee while Asfandyar ate halwa puri. 'I read the columns first,' he chirped at Asfandyar happily. 'Clears out my system.' A minute later, 'Asshole! Corrupt, clueless asshole! Motherfucker! As if we need more enemies! We don't need more enemies! You need an enema! You call this a free press! Free press, my ass!' He screamed as if the paper were an actual person.

He saw Asfandyar looking at him from across the table, a bite seized halfway to his mouth. 'I don't mean that as a sexual invitation,' he clarified softly, 'but these bastards drive me crazy.'

'Okay.' Asfandyar didn't read the papers. He was quite sure that if something important happened in the world, someone would tell him about it.

'You know what your father used to say about this free press we have now? He said it was too bad most people were too young to remember why those clowns had been chained in the first place.'

'Which paper did he get?'

'Oh he didn't get a paper. He said he was quite sure if something important happened one of us would tell him about it.'

Asfandyar was afraid to share how shaken he was to hear that. It was imperative, he reminded himself, to maintain an emotional distance. 'This is delicious. Thank you.'

'Don't thank me. Shaukoo ordered it before he left.'

'I'll thank him, then.'

'You're not as polite as you think you are, you know. Shaukoo says you hogged the blanket all night. And your fiancée isn't going to be happy when she hears how you snore.'

'Uncle…'

'Son?'

'About last night…'

'What about last night?'

'I don't…' He meant to say *remember what happened after the first two drinks*, but didn't. There was the distance to consider and the fact that being a lightweight would open him to mockery in the politest of male company.

This was not the politest of male company.

'Look, baby Nabi, all four of us, your father, Shaukoo, Ifty and I, belong to the raat gayi toh baat gayi school of thought.'

Asfandyar nodded. The slate wiped clean.

'Done? Shower and change first or the blessed reception of instructions first?'

'Instructions.'

'Okay.' Gullo folded the paper and put it to the side. 'First, I need to say that I am speaking for your father, according to the directions he gave us before he passed. Ifty and Shaukoo witnessed them too, so if you have any questions or would like to confirm, you are welcome to ask them as well. You are also welcome to confirm, with your mother, that she gave her blessings that we handle this.'

'You spoke to her?'

'I spoke to her.'

'When?'

'Before you came.'

He wanted the details of the conversation. Had she been surprised to hear from Gullo? Had she been sad to hear the father of her child was dead? He would ask her, when he saw her. He would not ask Gullo. It would be a betrayal.

'Go ahead.'

'Your father owned nothing but the things you see around this flat. The flat itself is rented. The lease expires at the end of this week so the flat needs to be emptied in the next few days.'

'How convenient.'

'More foresight than luck. He knew he didn't have much time. He's been, he had been, a tenant for over a decade. The landlord was kind enough to extend month by month, towards the end.'

Asfandyar kept silent. *Some relationships, then, he could maintain.*

'They don't make landlords like that anymore, you know. What about you, will you rent a place after you're married? Or buy one? Don't know much about what someone your age in your field would earn.'

'I make enough.' *My mother inherited her parents' house*, he almost added. But personal finances were a personal matter.

'And, of course, your fiancée can always move into your mother's house with you after the nikaah.'

Had he shared that last night? 'My father's instructions…'

'Yes. Sorry. Tend not to think in a straight line anymore. You'll understand what I mean when you're my age. So, your father's belongings, in this house, are yours to do with as you please. Whatever else he wished to give to others, he gave before he went to the hospital the last time.'

'You told me last night that he died here, in his bed.'

Gullo gave him a long, appraising look. 'We were joking. Then we also told you that he died in hospital, remember?'

'That's not funny.'

'Neither was the joke you told your fiancée. But I'm not rubbing it in.'

'I spoke to Lalarukh?' Asfandyar groaned and rested his head on his hands.

'Relax. You were perfectly coherent. And it was quite a funny joke. What do you call a Pakistani woman at a shoe sale? Raymond Davis.'

The young man groaned again, his fingers crawling, as if by themselves, to cover his ears.

'Do you want me to tell you the rest of your father's wishes or are you just going to moan like somebody kicked you in the nuts?'

Asfandyar raised his head. Sat upright. 'Please. Go on.'

'He wanted you to go through everything here, keep what you want, and give the rest to the Eidhi Centre.'

'Okay.'

'Except any alcohol you find stashed around the house. That you give to us.'

'Okay.'

'Unless it's the local stuff. That you can keep.'

'I don't drink.'

Asfandyar smiled. Gullo smiled back. For the first time, it was conspiratorial.

'The rest of what he wished to leave you is placed in my locker at the National Bank branch down the road, in a metal box. His life's savings, consisting of Rs 7,00,000. He lived off his pension, mostly, but it wasn't a lot, and rents this close to the sea are high, so he speculated, a little, to put something by for you.'

'Speculated in what?'

'What does it matter?'

'If they are his life's savings, why are they in your locker and not his own bank account?' Asfandyar couldn't help asking.

'Anis hated banks.'

'Is there anything Anis didn't hate?'

'Don't talk about him like that. You didn't know him and you have no right to disrespect him!' It was almost a shout.

'I'm sorry.'

'Ingrate.'

*It's a little hard to be grateful for twenty-eight years of complete neglect*, Asfandyar thought, but in the harsh light of day his internal life remained his internal life.

'I'm sorry,' he repeated.

'You better be. But I suppose it's not your fault,' Gullo sighed. When he frowned, he looked old. His mouth dragged his face down with it. Sunlight glinted off the fine white hair on the back of the hand he passed over his forehead. *Was he nervous?*

'Your father's savings are in my locker because he cleaned out and closed his own bank account and left the money in my care. He didn't just hate banks, he also wanted to protect you from the hoops you would have to jump through should you be required to collect them the standard way. You'd have to apply for a succession certificate. Before you can do that, you'd have to dig up your parents' marriage certificate, the divorce deed, your birth certificate, your national ID card, file an appeal to get a certificate that you were his legal heir in a court. Then wait weeks, maybe months, till the court put a notice in the paper saying you claimed you were his only heir and asking any other claimants to come forward. He knew you didn't know he was alive. He wanted to give you the option of not having anyone else know about it either.'

A notice in the paper, for all the world to see. All the people he'd told his father was dead. Old friends. His fiancée. Her parents. Her family. It would seem like there had been something to hide.

'Is there any other reason my father would not have wanted this to be public?'

'You can choose to go the succession route and find out for yourself,' came the challenge. 'He had his instructions documented and witnessed and notarized. The court could convict his memory of contempt – which would be mutual – and I might get into a little trouble, but you'd still get the money eventually.'

'I see.' A one-time pay off. He wanted to whip out his phone and do the math. How much was that, per minute of time missed?

'I don't think you do. I think you smell something fishy, and you should, because we're talking about a man who worshipped no master, no mistress, but the water. Your father didn't want to do it this way because he was hiding something, he wanted to do it this way because he felt you needed to have a choice in deciding whether you wanted to claim his parentage or his memory as well as his money. The legality of it wasn't a concern for him. He said he was following god's law in terms of leaving you everything. Man's law can go fuck itself.'

'Is there more coffee?'

'Instant in the cabinet, hot water in the dispenser.'

Asfandyar took a spoon of his father's coffee, a mug of his father's water, and considered his father's offer. Make it public, go legal, pay the taxes. Keep it secret. Calling a friend to discuss this dilemma was not an option. He had held, since those early voracious questions about his home life, a pattern of concentric circles of intimacy. Time shared was not confidences shared. The only people he could realistically allow access to this information, without fear it would turn into a case of Chinese whispers, were the women in his life. He already knew what his mother preferred. He told himself his fiancée, if he told her, would feel that way too. Plus, he would first have to tell her he wasn't actually in Karachi for business. He hadn't lied to her or anything. He'd just chosen to wait for a more opportune time to tell her. When they were silent at dinner, maybe. *Make it public. Keep it secret.* It was a surprisingly easy decision to make. He had to protect them. As for legality, who in Pakistan felt that was the norm and not the exception? He would choose anonymity. For Jehanara and Lalarukh's sake. *Not my own.* He repeated. *I'm not doing it this way for my own sake.* He pottered around the kitchen for another minute to seem more conflicted than he actually was.

'The succession option sounds prolonged and possibly

complicated,' he returned to the table. 'The other option might be better. With work and all, I don't know if I'll be able to fly down for a court date. And I'm getting married soon...'

'Of course.'

'It'll just be a lot of hassle, you know, and Ami probably doesn't want to be reminded of it...'

'I'll go to the locker today.'

'It might be painful for her to have it all dragged up again.' He didn't know what 'it all' was, but it must have been painful to be suppressed.

'Yes. You should shower and change.'

At the bedroom door Asfandyar turned. Suddenly, he wanted the old man's approval. 'Uncle, do you think I'm doing the right thing?'

'Passivity is the only sin. Making a choice is always the right thing.'

'Don't tell me my father said that.'

'Anis? No, Anis wasn't that wise. That, young man, is a Gullo original. Shower and change. I'm leaving. Ifty and Shaukoo will pick you up in half an hour and bring you too.'

'Where are we going?'

'We're going to bury your father.'

When he came out, the apartment was deathly silent. The warring birds were absent, possibly deceased. Across the gap between buildings, a lowered blind was a closed eyelid. Gullo had left the paper for him on the bed, folded to reveal a death notice. A black and white picture of his father in an open-necked shirt and a sailor's cap, one corner of his mouth turned up in a smirk. The old men had been right about the resemblance. Above the photograph were the words 'Anis Nabi, 1943–2013' and, under it, a list of mourners.

Iftikhar Salim
Shaukat Hussain
Gulzar Shah

They had known, all along, what choice he would make.

Animals used to concealment often freeze when exposed, hoping any predator in the vicinity will take their stillness for lifelessness. In the human world, the risk of recognition sometimes engenders a similar paralysis. The omission of his name from Anis's death notice had forced Asfandyar to consider whether the uncles were prescient, or his mother had made the decision for him, knowing it was the one he would choose anyway. Either way, he was predictable. What Lalarukh called his 'stability' was actually a lack of imagination, a plod through life rather than a hop, skip and jump. The thought of what the uncles, what his father might have thought, of his 'stability' drove him into a sullen silence even Ifty and Shaukoo's constant squabbling could not drag him out of. He had never wanted to be a risk-taker. But he was still indignant at being considered incapable of it. He greeted them politely enough. He even remembered to thank the latter for providing breakfast for him. Beyond that he would not be drawn. He smiled blankly at their reaction to seeing him sitting prepared at the table, his suitcase by his side. He was just a little boy waiting for the bus to take to school. Did he know the world was a dangerous place? Had he remembered to fill his bottle with sulphuric acid instead of water? He remained monosyllabic, non-committal, through their banter in the elevator about whether *it's a good day to die* meant the same as *it's a good day to be buried*. As the other two shuffled down the street to Shaukoo's battered Corolla, he remained a few feet behind them. To anyone observing, they would not have seemed companions. Their clothes made them strangers – their pajamas tapered gently to their ankles, his shalwar ballooned mid-thigh and collapsed, soufflé like, around his. He was tall and healthy to their aged and stooped. Where their faces were open, his was 'shutters down'.

Asfandyar wasn't the only person on strike. Across Karachi, transporters and traders, milk trucks and maids, obeyed the latest call to cease all commercial activity as a protest against, and mourning for, the bombings the day before. With traffic thin, pedestrians scarce, and beggars sensing enough menace in the air to stay off the main roads, the city lay revealed. Its optimistic roads. Its entrepreneur's dreams. Its financier's castles. Its Styrofoam roadblocks. Its gaudy roundabouts. Its sprawl and squalor. *What a colourless, characterless place*, he thought. He was suddenly acutely homesick.

'Gullo didn't rape you, did he?'

'What?'

Ifty turned around, looking directly at Asfandyar as Shaukoo chuckled at the wheel. 'Gullo. Shaukoo is asking that he didn't rape you, did he?'

'What!'

'You're very quiet. We were just concerned.'

'The way you were sitting at that table with your knees pressed together, like you were afraid,' Shaukoo said.

'Very funny.'

'Why are you so quiet, then, if it wasn't our Gullo's feminine wiles?'

'Maybe he's hungover.'

'Are you hungover? You did love the bottle, even as a baby.'

'Anis used to exercise by lifting you off the ground while you clung to it.'

'You used to find that very funny. You'd make him do it again and again.'

'And then you'd cry when he stopped.'

'You used to cry like a...'

'Say it, Ifty, he used to cry like a baby.'

*I was a baby!* Asfandyar thought. *Not a toy. Not disposable.*

'I was thinking that this is a really ugly city.'

'What's the problem, Lahori friend, Karachi isn't polluted enough for you?'

'Can't see any mobs burning Christian homes to the ground?'

'That was an isolated incident.' It was. Lahore was big-hearted, expansive, warm. Everyone knew that.

'If you say so. Sure this is an ugly city,' Shaukoo acknowledged.

'Hideous,' Ifty added.

'But it's an equal opportunity killer. And that's called civilization.'

Asfandyar didn't speak the rest of the way. Neither did his elders.

The silence extended into the morning. The uncles sat mute on a bench at the ghusl khana, watching the attendants wash their friend's body. They had done wudhu in the sink in the corner, then done Anis's wudhu too, rolling up their sleeves and panchas to reveal sunburnt, bony limbs as they washed the face, the arms to the elbows, the feet up to the ankles. Ifty's back had given out as he bent to wash the face – the bench was two feet below his waist – and Shaukoo had reached out to steady him. Asfandyar had approached, then, tentatively, but both men had waved him away as they retreated to their seat. After he had blurted 'No!' when they asked as they were leaving the car whether he would like to do the ghusl himself, they had not spoken to him. It was the quietest they had been. The two ghusl khana attendants now washing the corpse had not asked if Asfandyar wanted to help either, or commented on any resemblance they might have seen in build and features between the body in their hands and the man in the corner. He had retreated there after his first sight of Anis, shaken by it, but nobody else seemed to be. Had they seen so many corpses that all dead men looked alike to them?

Anis had been tall and broad-shouldered too. His long limbs, now lax and waxen, must in life have been like Asfandyar's own. *Is this what I will look like when I am old*? He was grateful the men doing the ghusl did it with the fluency of practice, so the awrah was expertly held in place as they washed each side, then raised the body upright to massage the stomach. It made it easier to keep his eyes away from the groin and what lay there. *It's natural to be curious*. Not about this, it wasn't. *It's morbid and twisted. And sick. I'm sick*. If Ifty and Shaukoo knew that he was fixating, they would pounce, mercilessly. Even his father, with the cotton wool stuffed into his ears, nose and mouth, might sit up, yell 'pervert!' and burst into raucous laughter along with his friends.

*This is not what sons are supposed to think about when their fathers die.*

*Why am I thinking this stuff?*

*I don't feel anything.*

He did feel something, though. He felt a failure. Cleansed, Anis was lifted off the bench and onto the layered shroud on the floor. Camphor was rubbed onto his forehead, nose, palms, anywhere the body would have touched the earth in supplication. *He didn't even pray*, Asfandyar thought. The ghusl attendants made to wrap him. 'Wait!' Ifty said. 'Just two minutes,' he added softly. The two minutes seemed an eternity. *Do they want me to do something*, the son wondered, *are they waiting for me to do something*?

Gullo entered. He was wearing the same clothes he had been wearing at breakfast. Had he gone to the bank?

'Did you find it?' Shaukoo asked.

'The doctor had it.' He knelt on the floor by his friend's body. The cohort rose and stood at his shoulder as he slid a slim gold band onto Anis's ring finger. 'It's done. You can cover him.' They rose together and bore silent witness. Asfandyar, in the corner did not feel excluded, but rather, invisible. *I don't have the right to ask if that was the wedding ring my mother once gave him. My choice*, he reminded himself. *I made my choice.*

It battered away the thought that it had been made for him.

In the parking lot, they separated again. Asfandyar, it was decided between the three, would drive to the burial site with Ifty and Shaukoo. Gullo would come with the body, in an ambulance.

'But what about the mosque? The funeral prayer?'

'Shaukoo?'

'Gullo?'

'Ifty?'

'Darling?'

'Are my blessed ears playing tricks on me or did the young man who refused to follow the ritual of washing his father's body just ask why we are not following the ritual of posing it in a mosque so people Anis never liked anyway can look at it and pretend to pray?'

'Your blessed ears are not playing tricks on you, Ifty, the boy who refused to follow the ritual of washing his father's body did just ask you why we are not following the ritual of posing it in a mosque so people Anis never liked anyway can look at it and pretend to pray.'

'It's a sad day,' Gullo said, 'and not because Anis is dead.'

'Young people these days.'

'What can you do.'

'Well, we could try burying them instead.'

'There's no call to be violent about it, Shaukoo, if the young man wants no part of this, we can drop him back to the apartment.'

'Maybe you could drop him, Gullo, you and Anis. You could tell him on the way, sorry we're going the long way around, yaar, it's just your son doesn't want to go to your funeral because the hypocrite in him is still alive.'

Asfandyar got silently into the back of the car.

The graveyard was just twenty minutes away. They made it in fifteen. The roads were still deserted and Shaukoo drove slowly, as if enjoying them. Qawwali flooded past the cracked leatherite seats and out onto the street through the open windows. God. The beloved. God *was* the beloved, the qawwals sang. Human hearts knew it. Beasts knew it. Stone knew it.

The billboards disagreed. The traffic lights, stubbornly red as the car coasted past them, remained unimpressed.

Every couple of minutes, Shaukoo would take a swig from a hipflask and pass it to Ifty. Asfandyar's chest began tightening. They were needlessly drawing attention to themselves. What if they passed a police check post and were caught drinking? The police weren't in evidence. What if somebody else stopped them?

They turned off the main road and began winding through narrower streets. Apartment buildings stacked like shoeboxes loomed over them. Shaukoo turned the music down. One more turn, and he had to brake. Flames from a burning tyre licked upwards in the middle of the street. A barefoot little boy was tearing up a cardboard box and feeding them. A group of young men in jeans and T-shirts stood next to it holding sticks, a few of them with scarves covering the lower halves of their faces. One carried a hammer. As they ran to the car the hipflask was slid quietly under a seat.

'Shit shit shit shit shit,' Asfandyar struggled to breathe.

'Deep breaths, baby Nabi, deep breaths,' Ifty said gently.

The car was surrounded. Shaukoo rolled down his window and stuck a hand out.

Confused, the young man waving his stick by the driver's door automatically shook it.

'I don't mean to lecture you, son, but I'm your father's age and I think it's my duty to tell you that kid playing by the tyre could get hurt.' The old man pointed down the road, past the bonnet. Everyone turned to look; the little boy capered closer to the flame. One of the youths trotted off and slapped him on the back of the head before dragging him back.

'You could get hurt too, uncle,' someone volunteered.

'Show me someone in this city who isn't hurt.'

'Where are you going on a day like this?'

'We're going to bury our dead.'

The one who had asked the question leaned on the car window and looked at the occupants. Ifty and Shaukoo, solemn, a younger man, traumatized, in the back seat.

'If you reverse, you can turn left and then right and then left again and you'll get back on the main road.'

'Thanks, son. Take care.'

'You too, uncle.'

The crowd stood watching them till they reversed past the lane and swung left into it. Asfandyar looked back to see the kid in the mouth of the lane, waving them farewell. *Wave back you idiot wave back before he tells his big brother you were mean to him!* He waved back.

Once they were back in the relative safety of the main road, he felt calm enough to speak. 'They could have pulled us out of the car and beaten us to death!'

'We don't beat old people to death in public.'

'It's one of our saving graces.'

'They could have beaten me to death!'

'But they didn't.'

'They could have!'

'They didn't.'

'Why aren't there any police around?'

'Because they might actually get beaten to death.'

'How do you people live like this?'

'Like what?'

'Like,' Asfandyar waved his arms frantically towards the windows, the world, the news stories he had read about Karachi come alive in the sense of a giant feral dog keeping pace with them behind buildings, waiting to pounce, 'like this!'

'What do you mean, you people? What're you? Indian?'

'No, Ifty, even worse, he's Punjabi.'

'Maybe if you stopped being so jealous of us, Shaukoo Uncle, you could get around to cleaning your own house.'

'Maybe our house would be clean, Asfandyar beta, if you paindus stopped flushing your shit downstream?'

*I will answer your question, oh Lord*, sang the drunk qawwal from the speakers, *but it's the Day of Judgement, so what's the hurry*?

'Has anyone ever told you you're really negative, baby Nabi?'

'Stop calling me that!'

'He's right. You just had a close brush with the fundamental decency of man and all you can think about is how badly it could have turned out.'

'It's not healthy, you know, that kind of thinking.'

'You could get ulcers.'

'They'd have to shove a tube up your ass to treat them.'

'That's not how you treat ulcers, Ifty.'

'Sorry, Shaukoo. I think I should probably change doctors then.'

Asfandyar's phone began to ring. It was Lalarukh. He

caught Shaukoo's eye in the mirror. He didn't know what he would say to her. He didn't know what he could say to her.

'Your phone is ringing, baby Nabi.'

Asfandyar put it on silent.

'Did you see what he did there, Shaukoo? He turned his phone on silent.'

'He doesn't want to talk to his women.'

'That's just disrespectful, if you ask me.'

'Nobody asked you, Ifty.'

'It's still disrespectful.'

Shaukoo turned the volume back up. *If you find heaven, bring it to the wine house. Put abundance in my goblet. And don't put my corpse in the wilderness. Put it in the goblet, put the goblet in the wine house. And, server of wine, don't close the door to your tavern just yet. Maybe the atmosphere of heaven won't suit me.* Outside, the air simmered in the heat. Fires burnt, here and there, visible as sparks to the eyes in the helicopters that flew overhead, but the fragile peace held.

The navy graveyard lay across the road from the National Stadium. The stadium, once an amphitheatre where the gods of the gentleman's game battled for supremacy to the roar of voices and the rattle of hundreds of bottles hitting against the fence, erected to protect the gods from their worshippers, was now a dilapidated echo chamber. Ghosts whispered in the stands, in the pavilions. Local league fixtures were still played; the teams named after animals most of the players did not know. The

Karachi Dolphins. The Faisalabad Wolves. The Peshawar Panthers. Cricket clubs sometimes brought little boys to tour the dressing room. The women's cricket team used the nets when it could. But the stadium, like the city, was in limbo. Nobody wanted to tour Pakistan. Not even the country that used to be Pakistan.

As a child, Asfandyar had felt envy when a classmate had told him he was going to a cricket match with his father. He had responded by developing an aversion to cricket. If cricket wanted no part of him, he wanted no part of it either. 'Did my father like cricket?'

'No,' Shaukoo said, pulling the car into a vacant spot on the curb outside the graveyard. Through the iron fence, grass, trees and low markers were visible. The place was clean and well-maintained, as spaces maintained by service personnel usually were.

'Too much standing around,' Ifty added, 'Anis hated standing around.'

'Did he play any sport?'

'Poker.'

'Poker isn't a sport.'

'You haven't been playing it right.'

Shaukoo took one final swig of the hipflask before sliding it into the glove compartment and locking the doors. They stood on the pavement while he walked around the car lifting all the handles, checking. Asfandyar considered pointing out that it wasn't exactly a vehicle that would be tempting to steal, but men could be sentimental about their cars. And he had already tagged Shaukoo as the prickliest of the three. 'Are they waiting for us?' he said instead.

A knot of men looped loosely around the stone gate with the names of the martyrs of the wars against India etched over it. They had spotted them and were walking over. As the knot unravelled, he saw there were more than the *three or four people* Ifty and Shaukoo had told him would be at the graveyard. There were about fifteen, or twenty. At the least.

'Yaar…' Ifty said.

'What?'

'It's your father's old crewmembers. They all sailed with him.'

'Arshad Bhai was his first cook,' Ifty nodded towards an elderly man at the back of the pack, so stooped with age he wasn't so much walking as being carried between the middle-aged men on either side. 'Haven't seen him in years myself. Thought he was dead. So nice of him to come, the old fool.'

'Isn't that Tuppi?'

'It is Tuppi!'

'I heard he was in jail?'

'He either got out or escaped.'

'You weren't expecting so many?'

'One of them must have told the others.'

'They're all here,' Ifty said softly.

'They're all here,' Shaukoo agreed.

'Who is that?' A bearded man of stately bearing led the procession down the sidewalk. The white prayer cap on his head matched the thick growth that bridged a span from his chin to his stomach, and he walked with his arms held out from his side, as if the loose kameez hid a bodybuilder's muscles. He looked like a man who had met old age and grudgingly agreed to let it, at the most, colour his hair.

'Motherfucker.' Shaukoo spat into the road.

'Your father's old boss. Well, the owner of the shipping company he worked for last.'

'Anis hated him.' Shaukoo didn't seem to like him either.

'Why?'

'Because he's a self-righteous bastard.'

'Because they didn't see eye to eye on several things.'

'Like what?'

'Like why it's okay to smuggle hashish but not okay to smoke it.'

'Why is he looking at me like that?' The eyes above the aquiline nose seemed to be fixed on Asfandyar.

'He probably thinks you look familiar.' Shaukoo stepped forward, down the sidewalk, to meet him first.

'Say nothing,' Ifty said to Asfandyar.

'But that'll be even more suspicious!'

'Okay. If he asks, say you're Anis's sister's son, from America.'

'My father has a sister?'

'He does now.'

'What if he asks me more questions?'

'Answer them.'

The men were upon them. The groups shook hands, dissolving into one long line. The men all seemed to know each other and the uncles didn't give anything away by making introductions. This is just another man who happens to be here. Asfandyar took their cue and worked his way from man to man, somber, implacable, till he found his hand clasped in an iron grip as his father's old employer stared into his face.

'Salam,' he did not let go of Asfandyar's hand.

'Walaikum salam.'

'You must be his son. He mentioned a son, once.' A klaxon sounded in Asfandyar's head. He tried to keep his face expressionless, as the man continued. 'Your father used to work for me, you know, for a decade. You must have heard him talk about me. I'm Khwaja Salman.'

'I'm his sister's son.' Asfandyar blurted.

'I didn't know he had a sister.'

'They hadn't spoken for many years.'

'Did they have a fight?'

'No, no,' Asfandyar tried to think of a reason, 'my mother doesn't like telephones.'

'That's unusual, for a woman.'

'Yes.'

'Where is your cousin?'

'I don't know.' He looked around, as if his cousin might have fallen into a flowerbed.

'What fools we mortals are. We think we know everything, then He reminds us that we actually know nothing.'

'Yes.'

Khwaja Salman was still holding his hand. Asfandyar wanted to get away before he asked any more questions. What if, by some strange coincidence, Khwaja Salman knew Lalarukh's family? He was being irrational. They would pass over it without incident. Khwaja Salman had probably buried more peers than the Hazara. He would forget all about this one in a minute. He looked alert but inside he was probably senile. They were all senile. Beyond the funeral was safety, and life. Asfandyar tried to work his hand loose by relaxing his own fingers, but the other's grip tightened.

'Where have you come from?'

'America.'

'Are you happy there?'

'Yes.'

'Where in America do you live?'

'Missouri.' He didn't know why he picked that. He knew nothing about Missouri. He hoped the other didn't either. Was it a city or a state? What if Khwaja Salman met Lalarukh's father at a wedding and described this man he had met from Missouri and Lalarukh's father recognized his future son-in-law?

'Are there good mosques in Missouri?'

'Very good mosques.'

'Whose mosques are they?'

'Muslims?' Lalarukh's father never went to weddings. He hated weddings. He hated weddings so much, he had almost refused to let his daughter have one.

'I know that. But what kind of Muslims?'

'Devout Muslims?' Asfandyar was beginning to sweat profusely. He could probably convince her to have a small nikaah, with no photographers.

'How is your mother? I will bring my wife to see her, to condole.'

'She's still in Missouri!' What if Khwaja Salman met his father-in-law at a funeral?

'Is she ill?' Nobody made small talk at funerals. That was the whole point of them. Intimations of mortality and the futility of small talk.

'She has cancer.' He managed to wrest his hand back as inspiration struck. 'That's why she doesn't like telephones. They cause cancer.'

'I've heard that. Is it true?'

'Well, she was fine, and now she's ill.'

'Did she spend a lot of time on the telephone before?'

'Oh, yes.'

'I have a son in Dallas.' Khwaja Salman said, proudly.

'Dallas is supposed to be a nice place.'

'It's all right. I've been, once. There is a good Islamic centre.'

'Really? Maybe.' Asfandyar began improvising ways to move the conversation away from family ties, as Ifty and Shaukoo moved further away from where he was trapped on the pavement. 'Maybe I can put the Missouri Islamic Centre in touch with the Dallas Islamic Centre and they can learn something.'

'You said it was a good mosque.' Khwaja Salman

was hurt. Why would the young man lie to him about something so important, his eyebrows said.

'Oh, it is. But mosques can always get better.'

'That's true. You know, I went to the mosque where Anis's namaze janaza should have been held. It is strange, but the Imam told me there was no namaz there.'

'Yes, there was a toilet problem!' He began taking tiny steps forward, but Khwaja Salman kept pace with him.

'What?'

'The toilets overflowed. Polluted the water supply. Nobody could do wudhu.' Asfandyar cursed his father and his friends. 'Ifty Uncle! Ifty Uncle!' he called desperately.

'That's terrible!'

'Oh, it was! Horribly, potty-smelling water, all over the place!'

'My god.'

'Exactly.'

'So where was the namaz?'

'Down the road. In another mosque.'

'I didn't see another mosque down the road.'

'It's very small. They just opened it. Very small. You can hardly see it. Unless you know where to look.'

'Who just opened it?'

'The Barelvis,' he felt he had a better understanding of what Khwaja Salman was actually asking now, 'Ifty Uncle! Shaukoo Uncle!'

'Okay. They're good people, the Barelvis.'

'Yes!' He was almost trotting, but Khwaja Salman had a hand on his arm and he wasn't so much moving forward as he was jogging in place. The pavement was a treadmill. He was bound to fall on his face.

'It's very sad what's happening to them. Muslims shouldn't kill other Muslims.'

'Nobody should kill anyone,' Asfandyar agreed. 'We should all live in peace. Peacefully.'

'That's what He wants, but these days…'

'It's very sad.'

'That's why I'm glad my son lives in Dallas.'

'I've heard Dallas is a very safe place.'

'It is, it is, I've been once, you know.'

'You told me.'

'How is Missouri?'

'It's very safe too.'

'Is your cousin in Missouri?'

'Asfandyar?'

'That's his name?'

'No, that's my name.' He had put his foot in it, he knew.

'What's his name?'

'His name?'

'Yes. What is it?'

'Shehzad. Ah.' The ah a cry of misery, repentance, a plea.

'Shehzada?'

The uncles had heard. The uncles had turned. The uncles were coming back towards him. He had never been as happy to see them by his side as he was then, even if he had only known them for less than a day.

'Shehzada Gul Khan.'

But they had stopped to speak to each other, Shaukoo

almost on tiptoe, pouring secrets into Ifty's ear, like they were lovers.

'That's an unusual name. People must have made fun of him when he was a child.'

'They did. That's why he moved to Germany. But I don't know where he is now.' He looked at Khwaja Salman with desperation in his eyes. The old man took a step back as Asfandyar put one hand on his shoulder and leaned into him, breathing halwa puri and fear into his face. If he wanted information, he would give him information. 'He's an electrical engineer. In Germany. He moved there because people used to make fun of his name here. He didn't come because he's afraid of airplanes. After what happened to my mother, he thinks they cause cancer.'

'But it's the telephones that cause that!'

'I told him that, but then he stopped listening. I had to do it on the phone you see, because he lives in Germany, so I had only just started telling him when he screamed and hung up. Now he thinks I'm trying to kill him and won't talk to me at all.'

'He sounds like a very confused man.'

'He is.'

'I will pray for him.'

'Please do. Please, please do.' He gazed intently into Khwaja Salman's eyes, willing him to ask another question, daring him to ask another question, but the man was appeased. He had received enough to mull over while he went through the motions of burying a friend. He patted Asfandyar on the shoulder, firmly enough to push his face away, and walked back towards the gate, nodding – as he passed them – to the lovers and their secrets. They did not stop whispering till Asfandyar walked up to them and crossed his arms and glared.

'Didn't you hear me calling?'

'What happened?'

'What happened? What happened? What happened is that he knows! He knows my father had a son!'

'That sounds like a riddle, doesn't it, Ifty?'

'It does sound like a riddle, Shaukoo.'

'What if he tells someone!'

'Who's he going to tell? He lives alone, his children live abroad because they can't stand him, and he has no friends. That's why he keeps going to funerals. It's the only time anybody will talk to him.'

'What about the others? What if he tells the others?'

'They're here because of why we're here, loyalty. You let a man take his secrets to the grave, when you're loyal.'

'So I just lied, shamelessly, for no reason at all.'

'If it bothered you so much, why didn't you just tell him the truth?'

Shaukoo and Asfandyar sized each other up. Asfandyar looked away first. But he told himself later that things might have turned out differently if Ifty hadn't, at that moment, said, 'He's here.'

They walked to the gate together, to greet the ambulance carrying Anis's body.

When the charpoy cradling the shrouded corpse was handed down, Asfandyar found himself helping to hold it. Nobody had pushed him forward, nobody had spoken to him, but a space had cleared between him and the one corner that had not been claimed by the most able-bodied of the others. He picked it up.

They carried the charpoy down a gravel path to a freshly dug grave by a tree. The gravedigger waited next to it, his shovel upright in a mound of dirt by his feet. He straightened, as the party approached, and helped manoeuvre them into a position from which it would be easy to lower the corpse. Asfandyar put his corner down and stepped back. Eyes played across the back of his head, he felt them, but he would not be moved. The gravedigger jumped down into the grave and spread his arms to receive Anis. Another man jumped down next to him.

The dead man's old crew made up in enthusiasm what they lacked in agility. Hands held him gently to raise him and then lower him again into the hole, with his head pointing towards the Qibla. The gravedigger placed the three hard clumps of soil he had prepared under his head, his chin, his shoulder, so that he was facing right, towards the house of god, and would not be able to look away till Judgement Day.

The men in the grave clambered out, the gravedigger helping his assistant gain traction by pushing forcefully on his bottom, as others at the tip above pulled on his arms.

Ifty tossed in the first handful of dirt. *To Allah we belong and to Allah we return.*

Shaukoo tossed the second. *From the earth did He create you, and into it shall we return you.*

Gullo held his in one hand for a few seconds and wiped away tears with the other. *And from it we shall bring you out again.*

Asfandyar stood, a stiff mute, at the back of the congregation that formed. Another worker appeared to help the gravedigger fill in the rest of the grave. *They shovel so fast. They must do this a lot.*

The old cook, Arshad, was at the front. Khwaja Salman moved up next to him, to the right, staking his claim to lead the prayer. The congregation, as one, took two steps to the left.

Asfandyar said the fateha too. At the end, it no longer seemed a betrayal, or forgiveness, but just something you did when people died, as his mother had taught him. What Jehanara in her home might be feeling, he pushed away from the thought of. The man was dead. He'd left him some money. It would be an act of kindness to pray for his soul.

*In the name of Allah, the beneficent, the merciful*

*Praise be to Allah, the Lord of the worlds*

*The beneficent, the merciful*

*Owner of the Day of Judgement*

*You alone we worship*

*You alone we ask for help*

*Show us the straight path*

*The path of those whom you have favoured, not the path of those who earn your anger nor of those who stray*

He passed his hands over his face. *Amen.*

It was done.

The men straggled out in twos and threes, none stopping to shake his hand. He was invisible again and he no longer had a problem with it. The day would pass from his memory. One day he might think of it and tell Lalarukh. She would be hurt that he had not told her already, but she would forgive him. That's who she was. The rose petals being strewn on the earth his father was returned to reminded him of her dancing at her sister's mehndi. She was so reserved and poised generally, but when she danced you could tell she might know abandon too. Rose water followed the petals. No stench would rise before the worms began their work.

At the gate, the uncles said farewells to the last of the mourners. Khwaja Salman loitered by his car, looking hopefully in Asfandyar's direction, but the son fixed his gaze on the tree under which the father rested, and would not look back till he heard an engine catch. Ifty, Shaukoo and Gullo waited for him shoulder to shoulder on the curb.

'Where's the car?' The Corolla was gone. Had somebody stolen it?

'It went for a drive.'

'Have you reported it?'

'It hasn't been stolen, baby Nabi,' Shaukoo smiled, 'we're getting a ride.'

A Hiace van approached. The wide, low windshield revealed a driver in a baseball cap and a woman sitting next to him, wearing a canary yellow kameez and a white dupatta draped loosely over her head. PRESS, proclaimed the sign taped to the bottom of the glass. The van pulled up next to them. The woman reached back to unlock the sliding door, and the uncles clambered in, leaving Asfandyar standing on the roadside, confused.

'Get in!'

They had, between them, commandeered the first three rows. He had to step over a jump seat, a tripod and two portable lights, to reach the fourth row, one before the five-seater cushion at the end, which was covered by a long package wrapped in a tarp, wedged in place by an icebox and two backpacks. The AC hummed at full power, the cold air felt a blessing after the heat and humidity of the world outside. The van smelt of camera equipment, lunch, pine air freshener, and something else. Familiar yet unidentifiable.

Shaukoo had stretched out on a seat in a front row. His sandals were off, his hairy toes dancing as he flexed his feet in the air, 'Asfandyar Nabi,' he said, 'this is my daughter, Alina.'

The woman in canary yellow turned and waved. She had wide brown eyes, wavy brown hair and in between an expanse of tanned, clear skin. 'Hello,' he said in response, waving too, and then feeling like an idiot. She must know he had just buried his father, he assumed. *What sort of man buries his father then waves to a woman and says hello?*

'Now reach back and open the ice box and hand me a bottle of water.'

It wasn't till he'd misjudged the weight of the icebox

and tugged it too far forward that he realized what the smell was. Camphor. *It must be on my clothes*, he thought as he pushed a corner of the tarp covering the package back to open the icebox and reach inside, *even in death my father has managed to mark me.*

# THREE

THE VAN DRIVER KEPT the radio on, tuned to Radio Pakistan, as the Hiace sped through the city using live reports of violence during the Day of Mourning to decide which roads to take. Firing in Nazimabad, vehicles burning in Sohrab Goth, Rangers dispatched to multiple sites as police unable to control situation ... Between songs, the radio jockey sounded bored. He was courting paralysis, as far as Asfandyar could tell, with the day's job of finding new words for flames and new ways for summarizing love. His monotone indicated he would much rather be reading news stories: 'Pakistan placed third in World Bhangra Contest'.

The roads the driver chose in consultation with Alina. Asfandyar noted her casual manner with the man and assumed he was an old, trusted employee. The roads they took were largely deserted. Once in a while a motorcycle would pass them, carrying two policemen, or a man wearing a helmet, and the occasional car. At a couple of places, other motorists were stopped at roadblocks while they were waved through.

'Why aren't they stopping us?' Asfandyar finally asked.

Ifty pointed to the PRESS sign on the windshield. 'Who's going to stand in the way of your right to know the ways in which people were cruel to each other today?'

'I hate that bullshit,' Shaukoo cut in, 'tricking people into thinking other people care. All these channels are owned by about five bloated bastards only interested in doing more business and staffed by whores, like everything else. In the morning they'll run programmes telling you how to live your life, and in the evening they'll run talk shows telling you nobody has the right to tell you how to live your life. And in between they'll do their best to give you a heart attack.'

'Seths and whores,' Gullo said, 'isn't that a board game?'

'That's snakes and ladders, Gullo.'

'Oh. Well.'

'But you don't have a problem with your daughter working in the media?' Asfandyar couldn't help asking Shaukoo, watching Alina raise a hand with a card in it, solemnly, to the Rangers as they were waved through another roadblock.

'Don't be ridiculous. No daughter of mine would sell her soul to a seth.'

'She's a freelancer?'

'She is. But not for the media.'

'But she has a press card!'

'It's a fake, baby Nabi,' Ifty told him kindly, as the other two laughed.

'Why did you have to go and tell him that, Ifty!' Shaukoo said. 'He's going to start hyperventilating again.'

And, while he was now too self-conscious to panic visibly, too determined not to give Shaukoo the satisfaction of getting under his skin again, Asfandyar did spend the rest of the drive slouched as low in his seat as he possibly could. He was too anxious to participate in the a capella version of the national anthem as they passed through a wall of siren sounds and a particularly dark cloud of smoke wafting across the road, too anxious to ask where they were going, too anxious to ask what might happen should someone stop them, too anxious to do anything but replay, again and again, the scene in which the shrouded corpse of his father was lowered into the ground and covered by hands other than his. That took him to an image of Lalarukh's tear-stained face turning away from Khwaja Salman at a nikaah he knew to be his own, and asking, 'Why did you lie, Asfandyar? Why?' His breath grew audibly shallow.

'Here,' Ifty handed a plastic bottle filled with whiskey back to him, 'have a sip. It'll help you relax'.

*I don't want to relax. I want to go home. I want to see greenery outside my window and hear the sound of nothing at all.* He took a sip and focused on just listening to his breath, willing his chest to rise and fall, rise and fall. They seemed to be taking the long way back, so the next time the bottle came around he took another. By then, he was relaxed enough to look out of the window and notice they were crossing a river, with a sprawling slum on either side. Had he crossed it on the way to his father's? It had been dark. And wet. He didn't remember. Then the van wound up and down through deep ditches and a long road punctuated with truck stops and tanker trailers – and he didn't remember that. And by the time they stopped to buy pakoras from the roadside on the outskirts of Karachi and hit a long, winding road that took them past warehouses and beach huts before turning inland and passing through low, grassy hills towards the plumes rising from the Hub power plant, he didn't care either, because he was asleep.

'Jaan, sonu, pyaray,' Gullo pinched Asfandyar's cheeks as he shook the young man awake.

The van was empty but for the two of them. The passengers, the bags, the icebox, the long package, had all been offloaded. Through the window he saw two grizzled old men in shalwars and banyaans manhandling them onto a fishing boat pulled up onto the sand of an inlet. Beyond lay the sea, a rolling expanse of water that smoothed into a hundred different shades of blue beyond the whitecaps rolling onto the beach. A sandbar extended from the left side of the inlet, merging into a coral outcrop from which a solitary fisherman dangled a pole. On the right, rocks rose to a cliff. In the distance, a giant armoured turtle seemed to have emerged from the water and frozen against the horizon.

'What is that?'

'Charna Island.'

'What are we doing here?'

'We're introducing you to the family.'

'I thought you were the family.'

'Oh. You sweetheart. We're all the children. Out there is our mother.'

Outside, he staggered under the hot sun and Gullo told the veterans loading the boat to open the icebox and toss over a bottle of water for him. They barely glanced at him as he drank. Only one grunted a response to his thanks. Shaukoo and Ifty were visible in the distance, helping each other climb down a loose rock rise. Alina stood at the water's edge with her shalwar rolled up, letting the whitecaps play with her calves. She had taken her white dupatta off and tied it around her hips so the wind would not flip her kameez up. Her hair streamed behind her.

'What are we doing here?'

'Showing you the sights'.

'I'm not interested in the sights. I'm interested in going home. People are waiting for me…'

'You can't go home yet, little prince, we still have some business to do.'

'At the seaside? What are we really doing here?'

'We're going for a boat ride. You like boat rides.'

'I've never been on a boat.'

'You have. You just don't remember. You have.'

'I haven't.'

'You were one, I think. We took you to Paradise Point. Ifty had bought a little dinghy. We blew it up and put you in it and pushed you and swam with it into deeper water till your mother started screaming at us to bring you back in. You were screaming too. But with excitement.

You thought it was the world's biggest bathtub. You kept reaching over the sides and smacking the water and yelling chupchup! Chupchup!'

'Is there a toilet here?'

'The world is your toilet.' Gullo pointed to the rock face Ifty and Shaukoo had just clambered down. 'Behind there.'

He stood for a minute taking in the enormity of the Arabian Sea. He had seen nothing to compare it to. It dwarfed the rivers of the heartland, his heartland. The sea – and Alina alone in it. She had waded further into the water and stood immersed up to her waist, silhouetted against the island. Her curls bounced up and down as she did, her delicate wrists glistened in the sun as she swirled her hands in and out of the water. He thought of the canal winding through Lahore then, in summer so dense with bodies seeking respite from the heat you could not see the muddy water.

'It's bigger than your canal, little Lahori,' Shaukoo patted him on the shoulder as he brushed past.

A row of dilapidated cinderblock huts lay behind the rise. Graffiti proclaimed the rise of the Pakistan Fisher Folk Forum. From the stench coming up, their only function was privacy to defecate. He urinated against the outside wall. A peek inside revealed nothing except debris, rotting clothes and garbage. He stopped at the top of the rise to get his bearings on the way back. A narrow road came down through arid hills dotted with wild grass to the inlet. Their van was parked at the bottom of it. The driver had opened the boot and the windows and the doors. *To get the smell of whiskey out?*

'I've been thinking…' he began as he joined the uncles knotted close to Alina at the edge of the water, but Shaukoo did not let him finish.

'You haven't been in Karachi for a full day and you're already thinking? How will they recognize you when you go back?'

'I've been thinking that I'll skip the boat ride. The van driver can take me back to … back to the flat … and I'll sort through the things and then when you come back we can do … that transaction … and I'll try to get a flight.'

'I wouldn't ask the van driver to do another trip right now. He's had a stressful day already. He might shoot you.'

'I'll call a taxi.'

'No taxis on the road today.'

'And no taxis would spend two hours out of Karachi trying to find Sonera beach either.'

'I don't want to go on a boat ride. I'll stay here and wait till you get back.'

'You can't. Too dangerous to leave you alone here. This close to the power plant, someone could kidnap you.'

'But you just said we're in the middle of nowhere!'

'That's the most dangerous place of all.'

'Why do I need to go on a boat ride?'

'We're just following your father's instructions.'

'I've been thinking about those instructions too. I haven't seen any apart from that note on the bottle written down anywhere, so I don't really know what he actually asked you to do, do I?'

'What did Jehanara say to you about trusting us, baby Nabi, before she sent you here to bury Anis?'

'Don't call me that.' It was even more embarrassing with the woman in yellow so close to them.

'I'll stop calling you that,' Shaukoo stuck his face close to Asfandyar's, 'when you man up and stop whining about things.'

'Stop being an asshole, Shaukoo,' Gullo shoved him gently away. 'Anis would be happy his son isn't a sheep. Look, Ikram Sir, we appreciate the patience and understanding you have shown us so far. We know this is hard for you, and maybe a little strange...'

'Ha!'

'A little strange. But these are the instructions we were given by your dear departed father, and as his family we are honour-bound to follow them. We would be much obliged if you could extend your patience and understanding just a little bit further and bear with us just a little longer and get on the bloody boat and let us get on with it before it's evening and the navy starts firing.'

'Why would the navy start firing?'

'Oh Charna Island is a navy firing range. But don't worry, we're between windows and if we hurry, we'll make it there and back before Alina starts collecting artillery shells as well as seashells.'

They left their shoes on the shore, hidden behind a rock. Three pairs of plain slippers belonging to the uncles, Asfandyar's black leather sandals and Alina's diamante-studded white ones. The two fishermen were not wearing any. They scuttled around the boat, hopping off to push it into the water, then using a rope to clamber back up the sides, once they were in deeper water and being carried out on the current.

*This is it. One last ridiculous thing and I'm done with these people. I will never have to see them again. I am calm, like this sea. I am clear, like this sky.* Asfandyar talked his mind into stillness.

The boat was long and slim, painted red with blue flowers. There were plain wooden benches along both prow and stern, a rusted outboard motor and a tiny shelter in the middle, constructed from iron poles and a sheet of canvas, with a reed rug serving as the flooring. The bags, the icebox and the package lay on it. Shaukoo crawled in, stretched out next to the package with his head on a backpack, and announced that there he would remain until somebody told him it was time.

Gullo and Shaukoo sat with the fishermen at the prow, chatting in a language Asfandyar couldn't understand.

'Do you know what they're saying?' Alina was on the bench opposite him, at the stern. Water dripped from her wet shalwar and pooled on the wood. The benches thrummed under them from the outboard motor. She had sat there first and he had followed after a moment's hesitation, unsure whether it would be appropriate. *But boats need to have balance, don't they? If there are five men at one end of it and one woman at the other, it might tip over. I better go and sit on the other side too.*

'I don't speak Sindhi,' he said.

She smiled at him, directly at him, a flash of white teeth between soft, pale lips, before turning to rest her chin on one shoulder and raise her face to the breeze. She thrust her chest out as she did. *What beautiful breasts. Stop looking at them. Stop it.*

'They're not speaking Sindhi, baby Nabi, they're speaking Balochi. Just because you're in Sindh does not mean everyone is a Sindhi. I know this is a hard concept for a provincial like you to grasp, but it is what it is.' Shaukoo did not bother opening his eyes as he spoke.

'Why do you hate Punjabis so much?'

'I don't hate Punjabis. I hate what their silence is doing to the rest of us.'

*If his daughter weren't here...* 'How long are we going to be out here?'

Shaukoo ignored him.

'It takes about an hour each way,' Alina said, 'so depending on how long we anchor, at least a couple of hours.'

*Why would we anchor?* But he didn't want to seem more lost than he already was. 'Have you been out here before?'

'Many times. It's so peaceful. I wish I could be out here every day.'

The rocking was not peaceful to him. The rickety boat

stank of fish. The journey felt perilous. The purpose was murky. Perhaps she meant the absence of other people, of human dwellings, of traffic, of din. Perhaps she meant the sea. He thought about why all the people he had met in the past twenty-four hours seemed to worship it, before realizing he had put her in the same position Shaukoo had put him in a minute before.

'It's very big,' he said.

Shaukoo uttered a disgusted snort and turned onto his side.

'What's the matter, little cricket?' From the other side, Gullo dragged his substantial girth into the shelter and lay down facing his bad-tempered friend. 'Did you have a bad dream?'

'Bugger off, hippo.'

'I know you're only saying that. I know you really want me to take you in my arms and put your head on my chest and tell you that I love you. That I desire you. That I pine so for you I can't eat more than four meals a day.'

'If only you ate only four meals a day.'

'I only eat those because your wife pays me to keep her cooking for your friends so she doesn't have to do other things for you.'

Asfandyar listened, fascinated, to the exchange featuring bottoms and bathrooms before their voices fell too low. Old men acting like young boys, talking like young boys. How different they were from the others he knew. But maybe he didn't know the others, maybe what he knew of them were the faces they wore. Perhaps, in private, with each other, they too remained in an endless loop of conversations from adolescence, heedless of the world around them. Heedless of pain, other people's pain, and their own. *Liar. You feel no pain for your father.*

'Are they always like this?' he asked Shaukoo's daughter.

'They're a little subdued today but, yes, they're always like this. It's nice, isn't it?'

'Very nice,' he said.

'Anis used to say people made the mistake of wanting to grow old with someone when really they should be wanting to stay young with someone.' She looked nervous suddenly, like she'd said something wrong.

'Did you know my father well?'

She wouldn't meet his gaze. 'Anis Uncle and my father were always very close.'

'What was he like?' He felt he could ask her, that curiosity might not be met with an arrow of mockery or dissembling. She was soft-spoken, polite and feminine.

'Um...'

'In three words. If you were asked to describe my father in three words what three words would you pick?' In school, that had been his secret formula for studying, reduce each concept down to three words, anchor all else to them, and follow the chains when put to the test.

'I'm not good with words,' she said.

'Try.' *I'm being pushy. Something is wrong with me.* He wasn't ever aggressive when talking to women. His mother had made sure of that. He'd been around the patriarch's handmaidens too long already, they had turned him into a savage.

'I really can't...'

'Alina!' Gullo said from the shelter, 'please go ask Ifty to stop talking so loudly. Shaukoo here can't get any beauty sleep.'

He hadn't heard Ifty over the roar of the motor, but she got up and did as she was bid. Asfandyar noticed she navigated the poles and the rocking with as much grace as the fishermen. He sat quietly in the sun alone till Gullo told him to stop courting heatstroke and come shelter with them.

In the shade, the breeze cooled the sweat from his body. Spray as the boat plowed ahead licked his face, so he moved closer to the centre. His lips tasted of salt when he licked them and he could feel the gel in his hair surrendering to the moisture. He could still smell camphor too. How long would it take for the smell of death to leave him?

'It's nice to see young people getting along,' Gullo said.

'She was telling me how much she likes it out here.'

'Tell us more about your fiancée,' Shaukoo still hadn't opened his eyes.

'Gentlemen don't tell, you old pervert,' Gullo smacked his friend lightly on the stomach.

'My mother really likes her,' Asfandyar said. *As if I'd tell you goats about Lalarukh.*

'That's strange. Your mother never used to like other women.'

'Please don't talk about my mother.' He was afraid he might soon no longer be able to hide how irked he was by their needling, their refusal to just let him be.

'Aw. Little Nabi finally found his backbone.' Gullo reached out and pinched his cheek. Asfandyar quelled the urge to grab his hand and twist his fingers back till they broke.

'You know, a Pathan would take your head off if you asked him about his womenfolk,' Shaukoo said from the middle.

'Well, I'm not a Pathan, Shaukoo Uncle, I'm just a pathetic little Punjabi. But I could try to take your head off if you like. You seem to want me to.'

Shaukoo opened his eyes and smiled up at him before closing them again.

'He's just grumpy because he's missing your father. He used to needle Anis constantly too, and he's using you as a substitute.'

'How did my father react?'

'Funnily enough, he'd try not to react too. And then one day he leaped up and punched Shaukoo in the mouth and Shaukoo threw a bottle at his head and then they just tried to beat each other to death. We ended up having to take them both to the hospital and all the nurses laughed when they asked how it happened and Ifty said they'd fought over a woman.'

'Had they fought over a woman?'

'Do I look like the sort of man who would fight over a woman?'

'I hope you don't mind my saying it, Shaukoo Uncle, but you look like the sort of man who would fight over anything.'

'It's because he's short, you know,' Gullo held his hand a foot off the ground. 'The little ones always feel they have the most to prove.'

'You know, baby Nabi, the last time we were out here, Gullo went swimming. Another boat trapped him in a net and hauled him back to shore. It took us a whole hour to convince them he wasn't a whale shark.'

'There are sharks out here?' Asfandyar felt his anxiety cock an ear, make it to rise.

'Whale sharks. Huge, harmless creatures that just swim around with their mouths open, much like our Gullo here.'

'But there are sharks too.'

'What kind of sharks?' He didn't know why he asked that. He knew only one kind of shark. The man-eating kind, from the movies.

'Very nice sharks. Who all went to English-medium schools and vote for Imran Khan.'

'Seriously, uncle. Are there sharks in the water?'

'Why else do you think there's no one else out here?'

'Sharks,' Shaukoo confirmed, 'and stingrays and barracudas and tuna and turtles and jellyfish and moray eels and a million other kinds of life. There's a coral reef rising near the island. It was thrown up by the tsunami a few years ago. A bunch of kids come out here regularly to scuba dive and see it. If we weren't in such shit these days, we'd have people from all over the world coming to ooh and aah over it too.'

'Yes. These are bad times for us,' Asfandyar said.

'Bad times for us, yes. Not-so-bad times for you.'

'Shaukoo Uncle,' he tried a conciliatory tone, 'don't we get enough of politics on television talk shows? Do we have to talk politics in our private lives all the time too?'

'I wish you would talk about it in your private lives. But you don't. Because politics doesn't touch you. It doesn't kill your children, and it doesn't blow up your schools. And when it's done doing that in the rest of Pakistan, it crawls back into your yard, under your charpoy, and goes to sleep. And if anyone comes calling and says your dog ate my life, you say this dog? No. This is a nice dog. It would never hurt anybody. Good dog. Good, good dog.'

'I don't sleep on a charpoy.'

'It's a miracle you can sleep at all.'

'Why don't you display the same judgement on the thugs who rule your city?'

'I like the thugs who rule my city. They make sure your thugs don't get to move in.'

'And, of course, they do it out of the goodness of their hearts.'

'I don't care if they do out of the goodness of their pockets, at least they don't do it because the Saudis tell them to.'

'How does it feel to have a leader who's in exile because he's wanted for murder?'

'How does it feel to have a leader who asked the

Taliban to keep their violence out of his province because his constituents have no quarrel with them?'

'Children! Please!' Gullo shook his head and wagged his finger at them both. 'This is not the time. Let's talk about something else. Shall I tell you what Anis did the last time he was out here?'

'I don't want to talk about my father.' He was angry. The words stuck in his throat and came out sounding sulky.

'You heard the boy, Gullo. He doesn't want to talk about his father. He doesn't want to talk about his mother. He doesn't want to talk about his fiancée. He doesn't walk to talk about politics. He doesn't want to talk about anything. He just wants to sit at the bottom, like a rock, while a storm rages above him. No surprises there.' Shaukoo rolled onto his hands and knees, tottered half-upright, and made his way to the back by the outboard motor.

Asfandyar took his phone out his pocket and began fiddling with it. He wouldn't meet Gullo's eye. The fat man got up and followed his friend. The young one remained in the shelter, by the baggage, and scrolled through his call list. He had no new calls. He had no messages. He tried Jehanara's number, then Lalarukh's, but nothing happened.

'No reception?' Alina joined him under the shelter. The spray began hitting her too, so she moved a little closer to Asfandyar.

'No reception.'

'I don't know if that's normal. I never use my phone here. The government might have blocked it for the day.'

'Of course. You poor Karachiites. All the violence. The lawlessness. No cell phone coverage. Must be the horrible Punjabis oppressing you again.'

'Have I done something to make you angry?' She spoke softly. Up close, her eyes were darker than they had seemed earlier, the whites clear, the lashes long.

*She looks so serious, so sad.* 'No. You haven't. I'm sorry.'

'Please don't be sorry. I'm sorry these old fools have upset you.'

'I'm not upset!'

'I'm sorry I upset you by saying you're upset.'

*This is getting ridiculous.* 'You didn't upset me by saying I was upset. Please, let's just forget it.'

'I've forgotten it.'

They sat together in silence as the motor propelled them through darkening shades of blue. The boat began lifting to slam harshly down. He realized how far out they had come and tried not to panic at how small, how ill-designed they, and the craft that carried them, seemed to be to navigate the vastness around them. She showed him how to sit with his feet against the side to brace himself. They swung out, past the island, and made their way around it, to the open water on the other side. The sea was no longer mellow and seductive. It didn't cradle them. It was angry, and powerful, and trying to break them against the island. He was glad he hadn't eaten recently. He would probably have started throwing up. As it was, his stomach felt like a ball left loose in his body, bouncing off his throat, his heart. The breeze now seemed a gale force wind. Alina, sitting next to him, was thrown against him several times. His arm brushed her breast once. She put a hand on his leg to steady herself. One of the fishermen yelled something to Shaukoo on the other side. He nodded and turned the motor off.

The men at the prow, working together, hauled an ancient anchor off the floor and heaved it over the side. Chain unravelled behind it. After a minute or two they stopped drifting further out to sea.

'What are we doing?'

She didn't answer, just squeezed his arm and scuttled to the side as the others converged on the shelter.

Ifty and Shaukoo pulled two large concrete bricks from the space below one of the benches, Gullo pulled ropes. The fishermen helped them fasten an end of each rope to a block, and then they took the other ends in their hands and waited, expectantly, as if for instruction. Gullo, Ifty and Shaukoo glanced at one another, then Gullo cleared his throat.

'Asfandyar, could you please move the icebox and backpacks to the side.'

He moved them. The fishermen moved in and, working together, pulled the tarpaulin-covered package from beneath the shelter and into the sun at the stern. They tied the rope around it, rolling it backwards and forwards to pass under it. Ifty and Shaukoo touched one end, softly, and sat back on their haunches by it, next to the fishermen. Gullo bent down and kissed the package, and then Asfandyar knew what it was. The affection. The length of it. The smell of camphor.

'Who did we bury?' He managed to croak out.

'An old man who died at the Eidhi shelter.'

'We stole a man's body? We stole a man's body.' *I'm a criminal. Yesterday I was a good man. Today I'm a criminal.*

'We didn't steal it. We bought it.'

'He was homeless. No family. He died on a pavement and ended up in a charity morgue. He had a better burial than he would have had otherwise.'

'And let me guess, you did it because my father left instructions to be buried at sea.'

'Yes.'

'I can't believe this.' It couldn't be happening. He was dreaming again. He was just having a bad, bad dream. Any moment now he would wake up and find himself back in bed in Lahore, with his mother waiting for him to join her for breakfast.

'Don't you want to say goodbye?' Gullo asked, gently, his eyes welling up as he crouched by Anis's body with one hand on the middle of it, as if it wanted to fly off the boat and he was weighing it down so it couldn't.

He stared at the old man, silently, till Gullo looked away.

The five old men lifted Anis and the blocks onto a plank pulled from under the bench, then lifted the plank and placed one edge over the side of the boat. The fishermen moved back then, so the three uncles were left holding the other end.

'Sleep well brother,' said one.

'Fuck a mermaid,' said another.

'Give our love to Osama,' said the third.

With one smooth motion they lifted their end. Anis Nabi's body, and the blocks that would hold it down till marine life consumed it, slid off the plank and disappeared into the water.

Shaukoo took a hip flask out of his pocket and carefully poured a shot after it.

They left him alone. He sat under the shelter and mourned without knowing what it was he was mourning. It wasn't that he had never known his father, it was that he couldn't un-know what he now knew about him: his friends, their crime, and himself. *I could tell Lalarukh the truth about why I came to Karachi, but I can never tell her the truth about what I did here. I drank. I dumped my father in the sea to be eaten by sharks. I buried a stolen body.* They had wrapped him in their secrets and now he couldn't get out.

Without a body in the middle to wedge the other baggage in place, it was more difficult to stay still as the boat, engine whining at a high pitch, fought to make safe water in the lee of Charna Island. His limp body slid here and there, his knees and elbows hit the side as he tried to brace himself, bruising, and through it all, he sat alone. The old men sat together by the motor, looking behind them as the sun dappled the patch where they had dropped Anis, and it receded. Alina sat in the stern, with the fishermen, her chin raised. She didn't look back. How much did she know? *She knew. She was in from the beginning. They couldn't have done it without her. I shouldn't be surprised, considering whose daughter she is*. Maybe she hadn't known till they were on the boat. Maybe they had used her as a shield without telling her what for. *She's just a woman.*

On the leeward side of the island, the water became seductive again. He pushed someone's backpack out from under the shelter into the sun – *maybe it has a body in it, a baby's body* – and leaned back and put his head on it. The sun warmed his wet face and he closed his eyes. Motes danced across the insides of his eyelids, snippets of conversation came to his ears from the front, where the fishermen and Alina sat. It washed across him, incomprehensible. The uncles were silent, pensive. Not repentant, no.

The boat's engine grew louder as the boom of the waves crashing on Charna receded. He opened his eyes and watched sea birds wheel across clouds. Raising his head a little, he saw silver fish shoot from turquoise water and skim across its surface before disappearing back under it. *This is the most beautiful thing I have ever seen*. He closed his eyes again, before his senses betrayed him.

The motor went off suddenly. *Have we already made*

*shore? So soon?* He opened his eyes to look up and check, saw the uncles pass one by one across him, and closed them again. If he needed to get up, they would tell him. They had been telling him what to do since the moment he had met them, and like an obedient little boy he had done it. *I am a sheep. So I will be a sheep. And lie here with my eyes closed till somebody tells me to open them because that is who I am.* There was a splash. A shout from one of the fishermen. Then laughter. The motor started up again. *We have not made shore. Maybe I'll never make shore again.* Shadows slid across his closed eyelids as the uncles passed him again.

'Is he asleep?' That was Gullo.

'Or pretending to be.' That was Shaukoo.

'Let the boy be.' Ifty. Good old Uncle Ifty. *He could teach me a thing or two about following meekly where led.*

They went back to the stern. He went back to his reverie. Floating. Powerless. Blind. *I'm a mutant infant in poisonous amniotic fluid, waiting to be born.* But he wasn't. He was Asfandyar Ikram, raised to be strong, by a strong mother. *I will not wallow. I will do what I need to. I will open my eyes. I will engage with the world. I will not let it swallow me.*

He opened his eyes and sat up, wincing only a little as his head hit a pole. The uncles looked solemnly at him. Gullo raised the hipflask in his hand in mock salute. He looked left. The fishermen were guiding the boat towards the wide, open mouth of the inlet. A pile of clothes, white and yellow, lay on the bench by their side. Alina was gone.

He scrambled upright, put his hands on the side and looked behind them. The boat swung alarmingly as one of the fishermen used a pole to push away from the coral. The water was divided into dips and swells, dark and light. *There!* Alina floated on her back, arms spread, riding a swell carrying her towards shore. As it dipped she turned over, went under, and came up swimming strongly, following the boat. Asfandyar's mother hated water. He had never been in a pool. The notion of swimming in a sea terrified him. *Her arms are so brown. Is she wearing a swimsuit? She's wearing a swimsuit. She's not going to die? Don't be silly. If she couldn't swim her father wouldn't have let her go in.* He could see her legs. *What if she starts drowning? The fishermen will save her. What if they can't swim! They're fishermen.*

He was so focused on her, willing her strokes as she swam, seeming to be pushed backwards one foot for every foot she gained, that he missed their own landing. The boat shook beneath him as they thudded onto the sand. He half-climbed, half-fell, out of the body into waist deep water and stood rooted there watching Alina till Gullo used him as a pillar to hold on to as he dropped down. He held his hand out to help Ifty down. Ifty leaned on Asfandyar too. *They are old and tired.* Shaukoo disembarked from the other side. They trudged onto the shore and stood together, watching the woman in the water.

She was in the cove now and swimming more slowly. Halfway through, she stopped and treaded water, then floated on her back for a minute, before turning over and swimming again. About twenty feet out she stopped swimming, turned around and, extending her arms before her, began walking backwards against the tide that tried to drag her out. Her slim back, shoulder blades flashing between spaghetti straps. The water washed off her. When the water was shallow enough, she turned around and waded. 'Shabaash!' The uncles applauded appreciatively and then went to find their slippers.

Asfandyar stood on the shore a few seconds longer, watching her yellow swimsuit-clad body – *she must have been wearing it the entire time* – till it emerged fully from the water. He realized he was staring and scuttled after them, embarrassed. *I was looking because I wanted to make sure she was all right. Of course, I was. I know. What a body. You're scum, just like these men. No wonder they seem to have adopted you.*

He took a long time to fasten his sandals, wanting to make sure she was dressed before he looked up. Two tanned feet with pink nail polish came into his eye line as he sat bent over, a white shalwar covering the ankles. He sat mute till she bent down to retrieve her shoes from behind him herself. Her wet hair brushed against his face.

'I'm sorry,' she said.

'No, I'm sorry. I should have passed them to you.'

She slid her feet into her slippers after slapping them together to get the sand off. Her clothes had dried in the sun, but were clinging to her where the wet swimsuit still covered her body. She smiled down at him but he just lurched to his feet and walked to the van and sat in it, at the back, till the icebox and remaining baggage was loaded, the fishermen paid off, and the procession began the long winding drive back from the funeral.

The driver sped through the outskirts of Karachi as evening descended, not stopping for bumps, ditches or goats skipping across the road. He seemed to relax a little when they were back in the city, and open shops and fairy lights where streetlights did not go seemed to suggest whatever danger there had been was behind it. The city had shaken itself awake. The roads bustled with motorists and pedestrians. Traffic policemen waved their arms nonchalantly, where hours ago ordinary policemen were nowhere to be seen. Twice they passed the charred husks of buses. Life swirled around them. Tomorrow they would have been carried away by the human tide. The smell of camphor was gone from his clothes. In its place lingered the scent of the sea.

They dropped him off at the gate to his father's apartment building.

'Shower and rest, son, we'll be back later,' Ifty said.

He slid the door of the van shut and walked inside without a word. *She never did anything to me. I didn't have to be rude to her.*

Inside the flat, he opened the windows. After the breeze on the water, the stale air seemed unbearable. He showered, standing under a jet of hot water till his skin turned red, then under cold water till it was soothed. He heard the beep of message received several times as he changed. *Cell phones must be back on.* Five messages from

Lalarukh, asking him to call her, telling him she missed him. One from his mother. *We can talk when you get back – love you son.* He knew he should call them both, say he hadn't been avoiding them, he just hadn't had cell phone coverage all day. *I don't want to.*

He sat on the card table and looked out of the window at Boat Basin. The cars whizzing by. *I'm waiting for something to happen.* It was a strange, new feeling, anticipation. *What is their next trick? How will they top their last one?*

When the bell rang he didn't open the door immediately, not wanting to seem too eager. It rang twice more before he opened it. It was only Gullo, carrying a small case and a plastic bag clinging to the oily packages inside. 'I brought kababs,' he said. His bulk moved forward and Asfandyar saw Alina. Her hair was still wet. *She must have showered.* She was wearing tight jeans and a short tie-dyed blue shirt. It reminded him instantly of the water. Of her in the water. They nodded to each other.

'Where are the others?'

'Ifty isn't feeling well so Shaukoo's taken him home.'

'Are there any witnesses to that?' *That was a terrible joke. What is wrong with you?*

'He isn't well, you know. Ulcers. This belongs to you.' Gullo handed the case to Asfandyar and headed for the sofa instead of the card table, sighing as he settled into it. He seemed smaller without his buddies. Incomplete. And subdued.

'Alina, child, bring me some water.'

She went to the kitchen and opened the right cupboard, pulling out a glass and filling it from the filter. Gullo told her to take the kababs out and serve them before they got too cold. She took the plastic bag into the kitchen and opened more cupboards.

*She's so pliant. She can dive into the sea without fear but she just does whatever they tell her.* 'Let me help you,' Asfandyar said.

He ended up rooting through cupboards like a fool for a tray before she smiled and handed him two plates to carry to the table. Gullo sat quietly on the sofa the entire time, his hand over his face, pinching the bridge of his nose.

'Do you have a headache? Shall I get you a Panadol?' Alina bent to ask him.

'No, child, I think it's just a touch of the sun.'

'Come and eat.'

'You two go ahead. I'm going to sit here for a while.'

She said they would wait for him to feel better, but the old man insisted. He sat on the two-seater where his friend used to sit with his hand over his face as Asfandyar and Alina ate. After a while his other hand came up too and his shoulders began shaking. Asfandyar put his paratha down, concerned, but Alina told him to keep eating. Her lips formed the words *let him be*, so he let him be.

When they were done they both rose to clear up. She told him she would do it, but he insisted on helping. He carried the plates to the sink while she carried the glasses.

'Asfandyar, come sit next to me.'

He did as he was told. A cold breeze tickled pleasantly

the nape of his neck on the sofa. No wonder his father had worn the upholstery down to a fine shine. The old man and the patriarch's son sat in silence and watched Alina wash the dishes.

'Why is she washing the dishes?'

'I've never understood why women wash dishes. They seem to like it. My advice is to leave her to it.'

'Is Ifty Uncle really ill?'

'We're all really ill. Sick in the head.'

It wasn't as satisfying as Asfandyar had thought it would be, the acknowledgement that they were not quite normal. 'You were just doing what your friend asked you to.'

'You're a good man, baby Nabi. Your father would have been proud of you today.'

'We'll never know, will we.'

'True. But there's one thing I can tell you about him, for certain.'

'I'm half-afraid to ask.'

'He would have stashed a bottle of the good stuff under this sofa, for when he was too tired to get up and go to the kitchen.'

Asfandyar reached down and patted under the sofa, heard a clink. He pulled out a bottle of whiskey, half-full, and shook his head.

'Alina! Glasses and ice!' Gullo perked up immediately.

She brought what they needed, pulled up a chair from the card table, and sat watching them as they drank. Not wanting to lose face before her, Asfandyar matched Gullo's pace. The fat man spoke faster and faster, not leaving room for questions or comments, as if he was in a hurry, as if he felt if he didn't speak then, he would never be able to speak again. He told Asfandyar why his mother had left his father, all those years ago.

She had been pregnant. Anis had been drinking, with his friends, his 'handmaidens' (he knew that was what she called them). He had staggered upstairs after they had left and tried to go into the nursery where Asfandyar was asleep, to wake him up so he could play with him (he loved playing with him), and she'd woken up and tried to stop him. The child was asleep. He was drunk. She was pregnant and needed to rest, not stay awake another few hours and put an excited child back down after his drunken father had gotten bored and passed out. They had argued. He had pushed her – later he had kept saying it was an accident – and she had fallen down the stairs. She'd lost the baby. He had fallen with her and stayed fallen, unconscious, while she dragged herself to a phone and called the neighbour to come help. She had left the day she came back from the hospital, taking Asfandyar with her. She had never seen Anis again or let him see her or his son. He had written to her many times. First he had begged her for forgiveness. Then he had threatened to take her to court to assert his parental rights. Then he had written one final letter, saying he would leave her alone and grant a divorce without argument if she accepted his financial support till his son came of age. His only condition was that his son not be told he was alive till the day he died and that his son come to his funeral. She had called Shaukoo and told him that she accepted – *of all the three, why did she pick him?* – and Asfandyar knew how the rest had played out.

'It was our fault, you know,' Gullo ended, 'your mother was right about us from the word go. We were bad company. We were bad company for your father and we have been bad company for you. I hope one day you can forgive us, like he forgave us.'

Asfandyar sat, mute, as the old man put his glass down and tried to stand up. Alina got up and helped him, putting a hand on his elbow to steady him as he swayed.

'It's curtains for me, baby Nabi. Alina will stay and help you sort out the place. Don't worry about her getting home. She's a big girl. She can drive. The landlord will come by in the afternoon to take the keys. We'll come by in the morning to say Khuda Hafiz.'

*I should say something*. But he couldn't.

She saw Gullo to the door and bolted it behind him. Then she turned the lights off in the kitchen so the low hanging light over the card table was the only light in the room. He resisted, briefly, when she reached down and took his hand and tried to pull him off the sofa, but she was stronger than she looked.

In the bedroom, he sat on the edge of the bed in the dark as she took his shoes and socks off. *Why am I wearing shoes and socks in my own house? This is not my house.* When she began to unbutton his shirt he pushed her hands away. She stopped and sat down next to him. The light from the card table fell into the room. Her hair was dry by now and brushed across his half-naked chest as she leaned in and kissed the side of his neck. It smelt of shampoo. It smelt clean. *She's clean. She's so clean.* She wasn't like the uncles. She was the opposite of the uncles. She didn't manipulate, or lie, or tell him what to do. *Alina is kissing my neck.* Alina kissed his neck again. She pulled his shirt off his shoulder and kissed his shoulder too. *Now she's kissing my shoulder, I'm just saying. Should I ask her to stop? Somebody should ask her to stop. I bet Lalarukh would ask her to stop.* He said 'Lalarukh!' Alina put her lips on his lips so the second time he said it he said it into her mouth. *I think she ate it. She ate Lalarukh.*

Asfandyar Nabi, nee Ikram, closed his eyes and dived into discovering how pleasurable life could be if somebody had eaten your fiancée. On any other day, perhaps, he might have resisted. His upbringing, his detachment, could have won the day. But he was in Karachi, after all, where you could buy one body, and dump another in the sea, and in the great, grand, drunken scheme of things, the only lesson you could learn from a city was not to believe too strongly in the sanctity of anything.

He didn't remember any of this profundity the next morning, when he woke up naked, alone, with blood on the sheets, signs of a struggle, and no evidence of Alina except a torn, blue, tie-dyed shirt lying forlorn before the open front door.

# FOUR

HE THOUGHT IT WAS a robbery, padding towards the open door and the torn shirt before it in his bare feet, only noticing halfway there that he was naked, battling nausea and a splitting pain in his head, his thirst sharp as a knife. Someone had come for his inheritance. *Why am I naked?* He made a u-turn and headed back into the bedroom to find his briefs and pants lying rumpled under the overturned wingback chair. Somebody could walk in. *Somebody already walked in*. He couldn't find his shirt. He pulled a fresh one out of his suitcase and put that on, his fingers fumbling to align the buttons with the holes. *They must have seen Gullo take the cash from his locker and followed him from the bank, kept an eye on us. They must have barged in after I fell asleep*. Maybe she had resisted. Maybe they had just decided they wanted the woman and taken her too. He picked up Alina's shirt and examined it. It was split down the front, as if someone had ripped it off her. Blood around the neck, and a large patch at the hem. *It isn't a lot of blood. Any amount of blood is too much blood*. They couldn't have taken her out bloody. Or half-naked. Somebody would have seen them. The chowkidar. The chowkidar would have raised the alarm. But if he had raised the alarm why hadn't he heard anything? They could have shot the chowkidar. They could have beaten him. They could have chloroformed him. They could have knocked him out and tied him up. He could have slept through it. *I should go downstairs and check. I should call someone. I should call the police.*

But he didn't know what had happened last night. He wasn't thinking straight. His brain was sodden. His consciousness stood at a crossroad in twilight, tapping its foot impatiently, waiting for his memory to catch up. He tried to push past his woolly mind, his dull senses and think logically. If he called the police, they would ask him what he had been doing with a strange woman and a bottle of alcohol. They would see it as an opportunity to extort cash. In the Islamic Republic of Pakistan, you didn't ever want to be caught with a strange woman and a bottle of alcohol. She wasn't strange. She wasn't a stranger. He could hide the bottle. He could explain how she was the daughter of a friend of a father he hadn't known whose body he had yesterday dumped in the sea. He wouldn't tell them the last bit. They would ask him why he had such a large sum of money with him. They would ask him where he had got it. His head hurt. He wouldn't say it was a large sum. He'd say it was a small sum, a few thousand, the abduction was more important. He'd say he barely knew the woman and she had been in the flat following her father's instructions to sort through things to give away. She was just doing a kind thing, for the recently bereaved. She was kind. She showered kindness. How could someone just waltz in and take what they wanted, just like that? He couldn't call the police. If they pulled one thread the whole thing might unravel. He knew he should call the uncles. But how would he tell Shaukoo he had let his daughter be taken, half-naked? *I hate this city.*

He pressed his tired eyes. Alina's shirt was in his hands. A bolt of her scent shot up his nostrils, igniting an image of her straddling him, tan lines on her breasts visible through his fingers where the swimsuit had covered them earlier in the day. *We couldn't have. We did. We didn't. That didn't happen. It did. It was a fantasy. If it was a fantasy, how do you know what she looks like without her shirt on? I don't. It's a fantasy. Okay. Why is your pubic hair sticky? I'm sticky because I was sweating. What does Lalarukh look like without her shirt on?* Asfandyar lowered his hands, dropped the shirt, and took a step back, as if he could back away from his own vision. *I'm just imagining things, that's all. Did you imagine yourself naked just now too?* That was when he saw the case Gullo had handed to him.

Brown leather, an old-fashioned satchel, it leaned against the left side of the sofa, where he had left it last night, untouched. He dropped her shirt, rushed to it and unzipped. Wads of cash in thousand and five hundred rupee notes, neatly stacked, slept next to each other like infants in a nursery waiting to be claimed. *They didn't take the money. What sort of burglar doesn't take the money? What do they want with her? What are they doing to her? What did I do with her? I had sex with her. I had sex with a woman. I had sex with Alina. And now she's missing. There's blood on her shirt.* He stood with his hands in the satchel, mute, his mouth hanging open. That was how the uncles found him.

Gullo and Ifty walked in together, expressionless, and closed the door gently behind them.

*They weren't surprised to find it open.* He had to hide what he'd done with her. He had to buy time while he thought his way through it. He had to tell them what else had been done to her so they could find her. 'Something terrible has happened,' Asfandyar said.

Gullo took his hands gently out of the satchel and steered him to the card table. They pulled up two chairs so they sat on either side of him. Gullo's hand was still on his shoulder.

'Something really bad has happened,' he said again, 'to Alina.'

Gullo massaged his shoulder and looked down, looking sad.

'Gullo Uncle, I know you left her with me thinking she would be safe and I swear I don't know ... I didn't mean ... I have to tell you...'

'We know,' Ifty said.

'You know?'

'We know.'

'Tell me, please.'

'You fucked up.'

'You fucked up big time.' Gullo said softly.

'I'm sorry I'm really sorry if I'd known this place wasn't safe I wouldn't have...' They waited, patiently, for him to finish, but he couldn't. He had to tread carefully. He was on very dangerous ground, the kind of ground that led to shame, feuds and corpses, broken necks and broken engagements. *I wouldn't have what*?

'You shouldn't have.'

Their nudity, the dark clouds of thought, eyes, hair, he had to hide it all and focus on the open door. Make *them* focus on the open door. If the uncles knew what they had done last night, all hell would break loose. Honour. Insult. Revenge. And these men were capable of anything.

'Have they been in touch?' He took Gullo's hand gently off his shoulder and set it on the older man's knee. He didn't want to be touched. His flesh might give him away.

'Has who been in touch?'

'Whoever took her. The kidnappers. For the money.'

'You think kidnappers took her? For the money? This money?' Ifty nodded to the open satchel on the table. 'How much do you remember about last night?'

'They probably couldn't find it so they took her. I remember talking to you, here. I remember you leaving. I remember Alina stayed behind a little while to ... you told her to ... she stayed behind to help me sort things.'

'I see you managed to sort things,' Ifty said, taking in the untouched bookshelves, the mess in the unused bedroom.

'I was very tired, so I went to sleep...'

'Where was she, when you fell asleep?' Ifty hadn't said as much in the last twenty-four hours as he was saying now. Maybe they had days, designated days, to speak. Monday was Shaukoo. Tuesday was Gullo. Wednesday was Ifty. Anis could have been Thursday. Anis could have been Sunday.

*I have to hide. I have to hide from everyone.* 'I don't know. She must have been here, outside,' he said. 'I must have been inside asleep and she came out here to sort things and they broke in and took her. Maybe they couldn't find the money, but they knew it was here and they took her so they could ransom her.'

'Oh, baby Nabi,' Gullo put a hand back on his shoulder, 'you're in a hole and you just keep digging.'

They knew something was off. They knew something was off, but it wasn't clear if they knew what he knew. He had to feint, distract, keep them off balance till he could leech their comprehension. 'What do the kidnappers want?'

'There are no kidnappers.'

'Then what happened to Alina?'

'Alina is in the hospital,' Ifty said, 'with a bloody nose, a fractured arm and scratches all over her body. She's in the hospital. Where you put her?'

'What?' Asfandyar's mouth stayed open, fetid breath leaking into the air till he closed it.

'She didn't come home last night so Shaukoo called Gullo and Gullo called me and we came out to find her. We found her by the door, on the floor, wearing your shirt and using hers to staunch the bleeding. She used to have terrible nosebleeds as a kid and pass out. Your breaking it didn't help any.'

'What? I didn't break her nose!' It didn't make any

sense. What had she told them? What was her cover? How had she explained the shirt? She couldn't have told them what actually happened. She couldn't have been that stupid, or that cruel. Was she that stupid, cruel, casual? Was it true what they said about Karachi girls?

'We got her to the hospital. They stopped the bleeding and set the fracture but she's going to be there for a few days. Shaukoo is with her now. There is some swelling on her neck too from when you tried to strangle her and they want to do more tests for internal damage.'

'Ifty Uncle, Gullo ... you have to believe me, I didn't touch her!' He had to deny everything. Deny everything till he knew what he was accused of. That was how they did it, wasn't it? All those people he knew and read about and saw on TV who did things and wriggled out of the consequences? All those people he'd looked at with contempt? *I don't have the right to look down on anyone anymore.*

'You didn't touch her?' Gullo said it without looking at him, looking instead into the kitchen, where the dishes Alina had washed the night before winked at them from the counter. 'It didn't look like you touched her. I came into the bedroom before we took her down you know. You were out like a light. Wrapped in your blanket like a spring roll. Snoring. She insisted we didn't wake you. Said you hadn't meant to touch her.'

*Thank god he didn't see I was naked under it.*

'But she says I touched her?' There must be an explanation for whatever she had told them.

'She says you touched her. Did you touch her?'

'Stop talking to me like I'm a criminal!' Except *last night Gullo was telling me how my father pushed my mother down a flight of stairs. And I know I cheated on my fiancée. Now he's telling me I've put a woman in the hospital. I should never have come. I can never go back again.*

'I don't think you're a criminal, son. I think you're a young boy who drank too much and got a little too excited. Maybe you needed to get some things out of your system and Alina just happened to be there.'

*She came on to* me*!* Just like a good old-fashioned man, blaming the woman. His mother would be so ashamed. *But she was coming on to me.*

'I would never do that! I'm engaged! And she's a family friend!'

How convenient it was, the notion of a family friend. Such a fig leaf, in clever hands. Did he have clever hands? He knew they did.

'You can't use family friends as a cover in a country where people still marry their cousins, son.'

'And we're not accusing you of covering up what you think we're accusing you of covering up.'

'I'm not covering up for anything. There's nothing to cover.' He had to stay calm. He had to stop shouting and listen, measure his responses, leave no room to be caught or skewered. He needed to know exactly what she'd said. They seemed to be saying she hadn't accused him of molesting her. *Would it be molesting? Or raping?*

*Focus, you idiot, focus!* If she had, their approach would be drastically different. They would probably be carrying fillet knives. Or they would have a gun. There could be a gunman outside the door. 'I'm not trying to hide anything. You know that I, apparently, forget things when I've had a little too much to drink. Please, just tell me what she said happened. How did she get hurt? I want to know as well. This involves me too, you know. You've been good to me. I don't want you to think I'd repay you by ...' He used his most earnest voice, furrowed his brow, and leaned forward. *Good. Sincere body language. Keep it up.*

Ifty and Gullo exchanged glances. Gullo nodded and Ifty spoke.

'Relax, son, we don't think you made a move on her. You'd have to be suicidal to do that. According to what Alina told us before her father got there, what happened was that you two were going through some pictures of your mother and father you had found in a drawer when you got very upset. You started screaming that you hated them, hated your father, hated your mother...'

'I would never say that,' he said flatly.

'Listen. She says you started screaming that you hated everything and she tried to take the pictures out of your hands so you would stop looking at them and you attacked her. She says you were out of it, out of control, like you were possessed. You kept calling her Jehanara and accusing her of ruining your life. She says she tried to stop you but couldn't and just curled up and kept very still and after a while all the air went out of you and you suddenly fell asleep. She says she used her shirt to try to staunch the bleeding and put yours on. She says she was just going to call us when she collapsed from the pain.'

Asfandyar was mute, shocked. It was an improbable, wild story. The bit about the mother was a nice touch. It put some distance between them. But he still didn't know how she'd actually been injured. Was she telling the truth about that part? Had he attacked her, in bed? *Did I really hit her? Did I break her arm? Did I break her nose?* Had he stayed away from women this long because he'd known in his bones what would happen if he didn't? Did he have a natural affinity for violence, like his father? Had he always sensed it? Had he known it even before he had seen two cats at each other through his window when he was a child and his mother had walked into the room, found him with an erection and sent for a maulvi to explain to him the dangers of the flesh and the importance of guarding against them? Was that why he'd said no to the girl who had wanted to be with him in college, because she'd wanted to *be with him*? Even if he had, surely there was redemption in the fact that he'd tried to fight it.

He had walked out of mujras he had been tricked into going to, saying he would not be party to disrespect for women. He had stopped going to his friend Ramiz's house because Ramiz said the masi was a slut, and she liked doing it with him, and would do it with Asfandyar too. He had fought it. *Until I stopped fighting it. And let myself go. And look what I am.*

This time yesterday, he had been sulking that he was

boring, incapable of spontaneity or risk-taking. He had been sulking because the men had thought that too. Now Asfandyar, splintered, needed reassurance that they at least still believed it. Lies. How they reshaped the world. 'Do you think I'm capable of that?'

'You've had a traumatic couple of days. A lot of things to absorb.'

'And you've been drinking a lot.'

'It's partly our fault, Gullo, we shouldn't have let him drink so much when he's not used to it.'

'I agree, Ifty, I agree. It's partly our fault. Son, we've been alive a long time, seen a few things, seen good men break under pressure. We should have kept that in mind.'

'I'm not that sort of man.'

'Nobody wakes up and says, "I'm that sort of man". And then he is.'

'Your father wasn't that sort of man either.'

Maybe he had hit her. Maybe he had broken under pressure and made a woman pay for it. Blood would tell. Blood had told. *I want my mother*. That childish voice made him sit up, disown it as his own. He wasn't a child. He was definitely not a child anymore. He had an ache in his groin muscles to prove it too. He was a grown man in a bad situation. It was here. He was in it. It would pass. He sat up straighter.

'You must have already called the police.'

'Why would we do that, baby Nabi?'

'Because I fucked up.' He used their words, bitterly and proudly. He was a man and he wasn't afraid of anything.

'We all fucked up.'

'We overestimated how much you were like Anis. And we underestimated how much you were like Anis.'

'My father didn't put Alina in the hospital. I did.' *Where had that come from?*

'True. But we got you drunk.'

'And Alina had been needling you all day.'

'We told her not to, you know, on the boat when she was being all sweet and helpful. We told her to leave you alone. It was cruel, you'd just lost your father. The last thing you probably wanted was some girl making cow eyes at you. But she wouldn't listen.'

'She never listens, that girl.'

*She always listens*. She had done nothing but listen to men in the time he had known her. Listen to their words. Listen to their bodies. *I only knew her a few hours*.

'Headstrong and stubborn,' Ifty agreed.

'She probably asked you some ridiculous question about your parents last night. That probably set you off.'

'I've seen men set off by less.'

'Remember that time some man told Taufiq he liked his shirt and he half beat the man to death?'

'Or that time some boy took Shaukoo's parking space at the dock and he tried to brain him with a wrench?'

'Or mobs. Normal people, trundling along, next thing you know they're a mob burning a bus.'

'It's the nature of man.'

'And timing.'

'The nature of man. And timing.'

How easily they did it. *How easily they tossed a dead man in the sea*. He should have been surprised but he wasn't. They had, from the very first moment he had met them, been unpredictable. He knew he was close to getting a free pass. It wasn't his fault because he had his father's genes. And the old men had gotten him drunk. And the girl had annoyed him. *She didn't annoy me*. The girl had annoyed him, getting in his face all day, sitting next to him asking him personal questions, offering solace like she knew him. She has asked for it. She had asked for it all. *It can't be this easy. It's not easy for her.* She was in the hospital. *She ate Lalarukh. What?*

'What?' He'd said it aloud, and Ifty was looking at him.

'She ate what?'

'Kababs. She ate the kababs.'

They looked at him as if he was crazy. He would have laughed if it hadn't been so sad. It was sad because after all the years of abstinence and waiting for the right time, the right woman, he'd crossed a threshold in secret, illicitly, without fanfare or celebration. And he hadn't just become a man, he'd become a bad man. And he was going to get away with it. But he wasn't sure of that yet. Alina might have covered for him, but there was another person in the equation, the trickiest of the lot, who had already demonstrated his contempt for Asfandyar and his innate desire to disembowel him for the simple fact of being Punjabi. How might he feel if he knew Asfandyar wasn't just Punjabi, he was a Punjabi daughter-fucker?

'You're kind to be so understanding, but what about Shaukoo Uncle?'

'That's the first intelligent thing you've said today, Asfandyar. What about Shaukoo Uncle?'

'That should actually have been the first thing you said to us, instead of lying.'

'I wasn't lying!' He didn't want to be back at square one. 'I just ... didn't remember at first. And I didn't mean to do it.'

'We know.'

'You don't have a mean bone in your body. Can see that a mile away.'

'It was the pressure. And the drink. It got to you.'

'Does he ... know exactly what happened?'

'If Shaukoo knew exactly what happened, baby Nabi, we wouldn't be sitting here talking to you.'

'We'd be on our hands and knees with a dustpan and broom, picking up the pieces of you.'

'Thing is, baby Nabi, Alina only told us the truth because she knows we're not stupid enough to share it with her father. She talked to us, and she's not going to say a word to Shaukoo till we've gotten back to her about this little talk with you. The doctor's going to hold him off till we get back, tell him she's in too much pain to speak.'

*What is worse? What I did with her or what I did to her?*

'She talked to us because she can't talk to her father.'

'Because her father is a lunatic.'

'A vicious lunatic.'

'Temper like a rocket launcher.'

'Who would kill anyone who even looked at his baby wrong. Oh yes. If Shaukoo knew you lost control and hurt her ... anyway...'

'So you're not going to tell him?'

'Of course, we're going to tell him!'

'We can't not tell him! You don't get injuries like that from sneezing!'

'And he's one of us!'

'But you just said he'd kill me!' Asfandyar felt the panic beginning to kick in and jumped off the chair.

'Yes. But we didn't tell you what we were going to tell him.'

'What're you going to tell him?' He paced up and down. He was petrified. Of Shaukoo. Of Lalarukh. Of his mother. *Have badly did I mark her? She didn't deserve a beating. No woman deserves a beating.* If his mother found out she would relive the ones she had received. He wanted to take a wire brush to his insides and scour Anis Nabi away. *Anis didn't do this. You did.* Shaukoo could press charges. He could end up in jail for assault. Or attempted murder. Or drinking. And if the truth ever came out, for adultery. *I'm not married.* Fornication, then. But the men never ended up in jail. The women did. No wonder she wanted to keep it quiet. Maybe she wanted to keep it quiet because it was awful and she wanted to forget about it. *Is that why I hit her? Did she tell me I was an awful lover?*

'Baby Nabi, you listening?'

'Yes.' He sat back down. 'Yes.'

'We discussed it on the way over.'

'We're going to tell him Alina was here, late, helping you like we told her to, when you had a seizure, brought on by the mixture of too much alcohol and an underlying medical condition.'

'What underlying medical condition?'

'Anxiety. Don't you have panic attacks?'

He nodded. 'I did, when I was little.' Now it was just panic waves. Waves of panic. *The waves off Sonera beach and Alina cutting through them in her yellow swimsuit with her legs flashing in the sun. Were her legs bruised? I gripped them. I squeezed her thighs. What is wrong with you!*

'You had a seizure. She tried to hold you down to stop you from biting off your own tongue.'

'Or choking on your own tongue.'

'Biting or choking. Exactly. You were flailing around, out of it.'

'She's a slight girl.'

'Your elbow hit her in the face.'

'Your legs sent her flying.'

'She landed on that arm.'

'What about her neck?' They had told him her neck was swollen.

'Her dupatta caught on a handle when you sent her flying and tightened.'

'She wasn't wearing a dupatta.'

'He doesn't know that. Men don't notice what women wear.'

*I do*. 'Don't say that. Say she had found one here that she wanted to keep and put it on.'

'Good idea!'

'Good man!'

'Why didn't she call him?'

'She was about to but we were already here. We called him as soon as we got to the hospital.'

'Where was I?' Was there any part of these people's lives that wasn't preposterous and convoluted? He didn't have the energy to offer an alternative, even consider one. Staying afloat was the only goal.

'You stayed here.'

'Unconscious?'

'No. He'd be angry that we left you alone, in danger of choking on your own tongue.'

'You came around and told us you were okay. But you were too weak to move.'

'You begged us to take her to the hospital first.'

'And when we came back to check on you we found you too ashamed to visit yourself.'

'You're all cut up about hurting her.'

'You're blaming yourself.'

'We didn't want to bring you back to the hospital with us because we were afraid of what it would do to you.'

'You were hysterical.'

'We didn't want you to hurt yourself.'

'You've tried to, before.'

'I have not!'

'But it wasn't serious. It was just a cry for attention.'

'This time, in the wake of your father's death, we thought facing the horror of what you'd done might tip you over.'

'Too many ravaged bodies...'

'Premonitions of the pointlessness of it all...'

'Stop it!' He was bent over the table.

'Sorry.'

'We got carried away.'

'Sit back, baby Nabi, breathe.'

He slid back and rested his head on the back of the chair. They were always telling him where to sit and how to sit. He groaned. Ifty brought him some water. He gulped it down.

'Are you sure she won't tell her father the truth?'

'She said to tell you she'll never tell.'

Code, for him. She had more to lose than he did.

'Even with this story, Shaukoo will still be angry that his daughter is hurt, but he'll probably forgive you, eventually. You're the only thing left of Anis. He loved Anis. We all did. We all still do.'

'Plus, he's a practical man, and you'll take practical steps to alleviate this unfortunate situation.'

'What steps would those be?'

'First, you'll leave town, today, first flight you can get, so his love for Anis and his patience aren't tested too much by the sight of you.'

Asfandyar thought that was the best part of the plan that far. 'And second?'

'Second, you'll leave some money for him, to cover the

costs of Alina's care, her hospital stay, and any cosmetic surgery she might need to fix what you did to her.'

'You don't have to leave it all.'

'Just whatever it is you think is fair recompense for injuries inflicted.'

'He won't want to take it, at first.'

'She might not either, when the painkillers wear off. She might want you to feel the hurt she's feeling too and charge you with assault.'

*Thank god they didn't know.* In the context of his upbringing, he'd done the worst thing you could do to a 'good girl'. And he was going to run away. *She's not a good girl. Shut up.*

'But we'll point out he needs it.'

'He's retired. His pension won't cover her care.'

'And if she's feeling vengeful, we'll remind her she'd wound his pride by making him feel he sold her.'

They waited silently while he thought about it. *Bye, big wedding. Bye, honeymoon. You don't deserve either. You might not even have them now.* He had pegged it blood money in the privacy of his head when he'd heard about it and he pegged it blood money now, leering at him from the open satchel on the table between them.

'Does my mother know the sum he left me?'

'No.'

He ended up giving them most of it, keeping only two hundred thousand for himself. They could stop at a bank on the way to the airport, they told him as he booked his flight, and he could change it into five thousand rupee notes. That way, it would fit in his wallet and attract no attention. He showered for the last time in his father's bathroom as they bustled about outside, packing his suitcase for him, arranging a pile of books on the card table that he might think about keeping. He told them he didn't want any of the rest of it. Not even the papers in the drawer. Not even the pictures of his mother and father in the other folder with them that had upset him so. *There are pictures of them together? What did they look like? Were they happy before he showed his true colours? How did Alina know they were in there? It doesn't matter.* They said he was a fool to let them go, overwhelmed, not thinking straight. They would keep them in a locker for him to look at the next time he was in town. *I'm never coming to your town again, and I certainly don't want anything else from that locker. It's cursed. I'm cursed.* He didn't say that aloud.

The shower washed the slickness from his groin.

He sat mute in the backseat while Ifty hurried into the bank. He was blind through the drive. *There is nothing here I want to remember. There is nothing in this hell-hole worth remembering.*

'Will she be okay?' In the domestic departure lane at Jinnah International airport he rested one foot on the pavement and asked before getting out.

'She's in a bad way, but the doctor said there was hopefully nothing he can't fix.'

'We'll know more when the reports come in.'

'Will you tell her that I'm sorry?'

'I think, baby Nabi, it might be best if we try not to mention you at all.'

'Except between ourselves, Gullo.'

'Of course, Ifty, between ourselves you and I can shoot the breeze about the prodigal son anytime we like.'

'How he flew into Karachi like a hunting falcon.'

'And exited like a cannonball.'

They got out of the car to hug him as he wheeled his case onto the pavement. Ifty patted him on the back, awkwardly, as if unused to physical contact. Gullo yelled at a porter who had swooped towards the compact suitcase, asking if Asfandyar looked like a lady. There were no effusive gestures, no promises to stay in touch. He knew as he walked through the glass doors into the terminal that they felt the same relief he was feeling. *They're old bastards. Happy to be rid of me. But they came through for their friend in the end.*

In the departure lounge, he stared fixedly at a screen showing highlights of a cricket match as colours and smells swirled around him and realized he was still hungover. Coffee. Perfume. Diapers. Sweat. Decay. Air freshener. The door to the toilet swung open as he walked past it to buy a Styrofoam cup of sweet tea. The scent of camphor made him gag.

He dropped the full cup into a trash bin and pulled out his phone.

'Hello?'

'Jaan! Where have you been? I've been calling and calling!'

'I'm sorry. I've been in back-to-back meetings. But I'm on my way home now and I'll tell you all about them.'

'Are you all right? You sound tired.'

'I'm okay. Listen.'

He paused. *What is wrong with you*?

'Hello? Jaan? Are you there?'

'I'm here. Listen, Lalarukh, I've been thinking. What are we waiting for? Why don't we get married next month?'

Dusk was falling as the plane taxied down the runway and took off. From his window seat, Asfandyar Ikram, once Asfandyar Nabi, looked down at the 'city of lights' before turning away. The sea was pulled up at its edges, a blanket over fireflies. *There are things in the deep. When I'm with Lalarukh, I'll never have to think about them again.* But the sea made him think of Alina, lying battered in a hospital bed somewhere, her nose broken, her legs bruised where he had gripped them.

He had to ask for a blanket to put across his lap.

# FIVE

LAHORE RECLINES BY A river, secure in her charms. Men pass through her. Their gifts outlive them. The Moguls left palaces, pleasure gardens and tombs. Birds nest over their bones. Her present owners too seek to mark her. Green and white minarets watch the sky, their bases tile-lined to wash what has happened away. Recently built roads are bangles on her wrists, every meal in her markets offered as aphrodisiac.

The grey in her skyline encroaches with hesitation. Unlike the virginal tiles of new worship, it knows it can't compete with red bricks blushing as evening falls. Sensual, ancient, wily, Lahore is all of these things and more. She has seen so many besotted young men they no longer register. What is a young man to be, she asks as she opens before them, if not indolent and besotted?

A young man in a rumpled shirt, high forehead, stubble on a firm chin, stood in the arrivals area of Allama Iqbal International Airport with a suitcase held before him like a shield. *Everyone is looking at me*, he was thinking. *No they're not. They're looking at me and thinking Minar-e-Pakistan.*

The denizens of Lahore that can be found around its airport after noon on a weekday – taxi drivers, families receiving prodigals, security, hawkers selling expired gum

– continued about their business. Those who found the young man rooted in their path calmly walked around him. The detour was no extra effort. In Lahore – home to verdant parks and trees that have forgotten more than most people could ever remember – to walk straight is to take no pleasure in ambulation, to insult the air itself.

A petite girl passed the young man. He cringed from a body blow. Lahore did not know, but her skinny shoulders had sprouted the yellow straps of Alina's swimsuit. The people around him were suddenly naked, the men standing to attention. He remembered to put one foot in front of the other, found a taxi. The suitcase rested on his lap.

They came down off the ring road straight into a campaign rally. A vanguard of hundreds of men astride motorbikes, two or three to a bike, the one in the back waving the party flag, the one in the front steering, the one in the middle – if they could fit one – trying to breathe. There were some in jeans and t-shirts emblazoned with the names of football heroes or American fashion houses, but most of them wore the stiff shalwar kameez saved for holidays, festivals, and occasions demanding a positive impression. After them, an array of three- and four-wheeled drives, the girth of the drivers increasing with the girth of the vehicle. Rickshaws, saloons and sedans, and in the middle, a four-wheel drive with an open flatbed. A white tiger sat there, stomach flat to its plastic pedestal, a chain around its neck, stupefied symbol of the Sharif brothers' Pakistan Muslim League. The taxi driver roared at the sight of the sher, honked. The honk barely registered in the blare of engines, hooting and loudspeakers playing party songs. The big cat remained impassive. Fervent supporters waved stuffed replicas of its magnificence in its face. Only the rise and fall of its chest indicated it was alive. The front of the taxi remained wedged in the rally as it passed, boys on foot climbing nimbly over the bonnet to run alongside the flatbed and the drugged beast. The driver remembered he had a passenger. Looking in the mirror, he found him asleep. But who could sleep through a spectacle as loud as this? He must simply, the driver decided, be tired and resting his eyes.

Would he like to follow the rally, the driver asked, that was the direct route. But if he wanted to avoid the rush he could take a longer, quieter one. The tired man's mouth asked for the quiet.

On most days there are guards at the entrance to the Railway Officers' colony in Mayo Gardens. They seek to keep out the gaping awam, the joy riders who come to admire the lay and ambience of a colony the British built to house their high ranking civil servants. That day, the driver knew, there would be no one at the gates. Every one of them had been pressed into attendance by one of the politically connected squatters in residence, he told his passenger. The sprawling villas, the lush grounds, were deserted, except for a sweeper pushing leaves off the road. It was the best light to see them in, the trees high enough to break even the strongest sun into shards that wouldn't hurt the eyes, the peepal sentinels, the fruit-laden belles.

He sighed and slowed, rolling his window down to let breeze and birdsong into his heart, which opened so wide he thought he might fall into it and drown.

In the rear-view mirror, the man in the back seat still had his eyes closed. The driver felt hurt, offended that the information, the visual feast his skill at route selection had placed before his passenger, were being bluntly refused. He took offense for the trees too, and the birds, and the light itself. His heart closed. The taxi accelerated. A maid dusting by the second-floor window of a bungalow rushed to tell her mistress the gatepost had clearly been deserted again. There would be words when the master returned. She would grace the absent guardians with a few of her own on her way home later, if they had returned by then. It was an idyllic space, the colony. Did they not know how vital it was to remain possessive of it?

They came out ahead of the rally on Walton Road. Traffic fled before it. Anarchic at the best of times, panic at being caught in the merry mob behind elevated it to chaos. The donkeys and oxen carts began pulling to the side of the road, the drivers settling down for tea and patience. The cars and bikes sped ahead. Only the buses were unmoved in their bus lanes. They were new and still believed in the supremacy of time.

The taxi left the din and fumes and honking and donkeys and swung into a narrow lane. Open front shops and stalls lined both sides. Shampoo packs, lotas, parandas, industrial-strength bleach fell like hair over their vacuous faces. Men, women and children ambled to the side as the taxi crept forward, some grudgingly, some happily. Conversations flowed. Laughter pealed. Even the curmudgeons had a smile prepared. In Lahore, in festive season, you never knew when you might need it. And this election was the most festive of all. Imran Khan's Pakistan Tehrik-e-Insaaf was mounting a challenge to the long-serving incumbents, and nothing elevated Punjabis more than a contest with other Punjabis.

At the end of the bazaar, the taxi cut into a service road and then through an improvised arch into a leafy neighbourhood. Over the low boundary wall of a cricket field, the driver saw children dance as a nipping in-swinger scalped a batsman. An elderly couple stepped gingerly over a puddle forming at the foot of a driveway as a burly woman washed it. The woman's head covered by a white dupatta held in place by her protruding ears, her shalwar pulled up to reveal thick ankles and spavined feet. The taxi driver slowed to look her up and down. She ignored him and kept pouring from the bucket onto the dust.

The generosity of the passenger's tip as he dropped him at the gate of a house made it easy for the driver to forget the miserliness of his company. As he ran over the day's encounters with his wife late at night, he cast him as a depleted man, not a surly one. He must have been away a long time, the man told his wife, no less than three people had come out to greet him.

Wahab, one half of the elderly couple that had been with Jehanara's family for decades, had opened the gate to the bungalow. He had been holding little Asfandyar's hand, and belongings, since the time they had walked down the street to the corner shop to buy Fruta Chews. They didn't make Fruta Chews anymore. The corner shop was long gone too. Four brothers had lived behind and owned it together. Their sons had wanted to demolish the shop and the joint family system and build an arcade in its place. There was a wall around an empty plot where they had lived, once, and the brothers in court fighting a case about commercial land use in residential areas. That was how long Wahab had been holding little Asfandyar's hand and belongings, so he was hurt at being denied the suitcase.

Standing on the steps outside the front door where the taxi driver had glimpsed them through the half-open gate, Wahab's wife Shabbo and Jehanara watched the silent struggle between the two men with amusement. It was sweet of Asfandyar, they both thought, to try to spare the old man even the lightest of burdens. That had always been his way, they knew, whatever Wahab thought.

They were a striking couple, the women. Jehanara in an earth-toned ensemble of long kameez and voluminous shalwar, her gray hair in a thick, neat plait over her shoulder, meticulous centre parting. Shabbo – twenty years younger than her septuagenarian husband – rotund and alert next to her, poised on the balls of her feet, the bright print of her wrap-around dupatta making it look like a bouquet had exploded across her chest.

Decades of proximity had bred between the women an easy familiarity, but Shabbo still knew to wait for her employer to greet her son – a hand at the back of his neck drawing his head into her shoulder, the boy bent like a paper clip with the suitcase wedged awkwardly between them – before stepping forward to make her own greeting. She took his face between her hands and he leaned down to accept the kiss on the forehead. She felt he had closed his eyes as he usually did, but she raised his head to find them wide open.

If he had asked for a few minutes to freshen up they would have given it to him. But he put the suitcase down by the door – Wahab pounced on it immediately and staggered down the corridor to his bedroom with it – and followed them meekly into the kitchen. It was lunchtime. Old people did not like to wait. They had made his favourite dish, aloo gosht, and Shabbo ladled it into the serving dish still steaming from the heat of the gas stove while he washed his hands at the kitchen sink. Jehanara had already taken her place at the head of the table. He sat adjacent to her, looking around with a wide-eyed stare Shabbo could not recall seeing on his face, as if he had never seen the room before.

It was a big kitchen, recently refurbished from Asfandyar's earnings. The cabinets were light pine, shades lighter than the bark of the chikoo and mango trees visible in the backyard through the windows along the outside wall. Pale green tiles with a blue geometric pattern warded anywhere water might fall or oil might splatter. A matka sat on the counter next to the Nestle water dispenser. The old folk preferred meetha pani, still. And on a stand by the door was the newest addition of all, a small TV. There was a big flat screen in her bedroom, but Jehanara would now watch the latest dramas in the kitchen as Shabbo cooked. They talked about the characters as if they knew them.

The potatoes lay drowned in the ghee. Arranged prominently was the mutton femur, Asfandyar's perennial first choice. Jehanara ladled it onto his plate for him. As she watched him begin to eat she chomped on discs of mooli from the salad plate. She heard the sound of her own molars chomping the vegetable into pulp and, embarrassed, stopped chewing for a second before starting again. He was her son, not a stranger inhibition should be practiced before.

He hadn't sucked the marrow from the bone. She reached across and used her finger to push it around his plate and tell him so. He looked at her, blank faced, before lifting it to his mouth. She got the distinct impression he had said he didn't want it aloud, but the only thing between his lips was the bone.

She told Shabbo the butcher hadn't cut the meat properly. Look? She skated around her son's plate some more then withdrew, wiping her hands with a tissue before putting them in her lap. Her fingers were short and stubby. Fat bulged over her gold-and-white gold bands. None of them were on the ring digit. Asfandyar, she realized, was staring at them.

Was he not enjoying the food? He said he was. He

said he was tired. She said he was too young to be tired. He said she was right and ate another helping. She felt he had, as ever, said the kind thing to spare her feelings. A wave of love for her son's gentle goodness washed over her, leaving her breathless.

She marvelled at the physical perfection of him, the clear, wide eyes, the solid bones, the perfectly proportioned form, black hair curling on his forearms where he had pushed his sleeves up. She thought, as mothers of sons do, of the miracle by which a female body can produce a flawless replica of its anti-thesis. He was a triumph, her son, as much a hero as that Fawad from the TV. He deserved as rewarding a life as the other boy. He deserved better than what his father would have given him. He must have come back from the burial thinking the same. She would ask him about it. He would tell her, now that he had seen what the alternative would have been, that she had been right to walk away.

She would ask him about it later. He was tired, her boy.

The commercial break ended and the drama the women had been watching came back. Shabbo – back from having served her husband on his charpoy in the drive outside – turned the volume back up after a nod from Jehanara, then settled onto her moora by the table with a small plate on her lap to watch alongside. There had been a cliffhanger before the break. Fawad's snooty woman boss had tried to sabotage his relationship with his fiancée by sending him on an extended business trip to the Netherlands. Women had thrown themselves at him, as ever, and he had had no shield but his principles. He hadn't known, though, that one of his colleagues, at his woman boss's bidding, had quietly taken pictures of him explaining to a white waitress he had stopped from throwing herself off a bridge that he was engaged. He was innocent, but blackmail was inevitable.

Asfandyar grew restless next to Jehanara. She saw him take a few sharp breaths, heard his chair legs squeak as he began to rock back and forth a little. Did he mind if they kept watching the drama, she asked. He was tired, wasn't he, and they could always talk later.

She reached out to stroke his hair as he got up. He flinched, as if afraid to be touched. His mother scolded him, told him to stand still and submit. He was her child and it was her right to touch him.

Outside, Lahore at siesta time was comatose and beautiful. It registered the boy-man's retreat as it had registered his arousal, with indifference. The wounds of one household merged into a deeper wound, the silence of stones and the stone people between them. No drugged tiger could lick them awake.

Asfandyar sat on the edge of his bed and looked at it through a stranger's eyes. It was a slim, single bed. There was no room there for a man who might like to spread out a little, who might not sleep alone. The lampshade on the bedside was striped silk, with a fringe. Old. It predated him. Lalarukh had laughed at it the one time she had been in his room. Jehanara and Shabbo had gone shopping for clothes for his engagement ceremony. But Wahab had told on them and she had never been to Jehanara's house unsupervised since. A calendar from work hung from a nail on the wall, next to a framed print of doves. He'd never had time for décor or art. His mother had told him he didn't need to because that was what women did. Men provided the walls. There was a carpet from the eighties, green and yellow polka dots. He didn't like green. Along one wall stood antique almirahs. In them, he would find his clothes ironed and hung neatly. His socks laid next to each other in the drawers. His underwear stacked according to colour. His few ties on a hanger. He wondered if his mother still stood over Shabbo, to make sure the other woman got everything right. You have to watch the servants, she would say to him when he was a child, you have to watch everyone.

He knew he was at home but he felt he could never be home again. He had left a boy, he knew, and come back across a different threshold. How was he to slip back into old shoes?

'Asfandyar?' His mother was at the door. The drama must have ended. Or she had sensed his unease and wished to mine it. She would want to talk to him. She would want to know what had happened, every detail. She would discuss it with Shabbo, afterwards, and they would dissect his account with the ruthless eye of women who lived vicariously. A boy would lie, to protect them and himself. What would a man do?

He was afraid to speak. He didn't know who would answer.

He closed his eyes and felt Alina's mouth at the base of his throat. Heat radiated from it, a stone thrown in water, ripples like her body in the water.

'Asfandyar?' She would turn the knob in a second.

He couldn't let her in. He wasn't alone. The other place – where evil lived – was with him, and Alina in it. He got down on his hands and knees to peek at the sliver of light under his door, seeing only the shadow in it.

He took his shoes off and lay down and tried to get comfortable. With both eyes closed he felt Alina was on top of him again.

Her right breast was larger than her left. Marks ran across her stomach, tyre tracks on a dirt road. Something had passed there before. She was scarred. Maybe her father had hurt her.

Asfandyar had been raised on recycled words, to recycle them further. He could not make new ones. So he didn't have the ones to describe what was happening to his body, why the blood ran amok so, why the limbs dived, why one woman had stirred him in a way another couldn't, why he couldn't speak. Why he felt he was finally awake and no lullaby from his mother could put him back to sleep.

With his eyes open, she was in his room even if she

wasn't. In the order, in the print, in the carpet, in the keyhole.

He closed his eyes again. Alina's head on the pillow next to him. She smiled. He felt punched in the face by the tight fist of her joy.

He opened his eyes and stared at the doorknob.

But the knob didn't turn. Outside, a light footfall as his mother walked away.

He realized he hadn't even thought to lock the door. It didn't matter because he was trapped anyway. And he didn't have the words to ask for help.

Anis was sitting on the edge of his bed. 'I'll help you,' he said. 'I'll teach you what she can't,' he said. 'I'll tell you what you need to say.'

# SIX

STATION HOUSE OFFICER MOIN was an earnest man. He had learnt as a child the risks of a joke. A riff on his bully of an older brother's unfortunate death in a water tank had earned him a rope-anchored suspension of his own. His grandfather had hung him upside down over the tank till he felt the child understood the gravity of the death of a firstborn. He spent the ensuing decades cultivating an immunity to humour. Now someone, he felt, struggling to think over the commotion down the corridor, was trying to expose him to it today.

'Tell me again,' he said, 'why today of all days there is a riot in my holding cell?'

Constables Ikram and Billa shuffled their feet and stared straight ahead, veterans of long silences. SHO Moin threatened to extend their shift every day for a week. Billa looked at Ikram, Ikram looked at Billa.

'We told you sir, it's not a riot.'

'I can hear slogans.'

'They're not slogans, sir, they're couplets. Poetry.'

'That's how it starts you know, people throw poetry around and then they're throwing bricks. I don't like it. And why is it happening in my jail? Those people should be thinking about the consequences of their actions. In silence.'

'We told you already, sir, it was the drunk who started it,' Billa said.

'The drunk you picked up from the sidewalk?'

'Yes, sir.'

'Tell me again how he came to your attention. I could read the FIR, but I see you haven't registered it yet.' SHO Moin embodied the classic need of the humourless for detail. A lack of detail left space for imagination to strike and SHO Moin was as suspicious of imagination as he was of humour. And poetry. They were, he felt, the enemies of efficiency. As were the two men standing before him. The drunk had been creating chaos in his jail for two hours, and they hadn't even written their report yet. He would have pressed them further, but his cell phone rang. It was the deputy superintendent police calling, again, SHO Moin knew. He had no option but to answer it. A ranking Rangers official, who had probably just been publicly humiliated by a ranking army officer, had probably just publicly humiliated the DSP and he wanted to feel like a man again. Police work in Karachi was no longer about passing the buck but passing the pain in the ass down the ranks. The constables made their escape as he winced. In the corridor outside the SHO's office, the two argued briefly about which of them would write the report. They agreed that, whichever neck the sword of composition fell on, certain details of the morning's events needed to be left out. These included the exact details of how the drunk had ended up in their custody.

Constables Ikram and Billa had been sputtering along

the very outskirts of their usual beat around Jinnah International Airport on Billa's second-hand Honda CD70, trying to ignore the sounds of explosions and firing coming from it, the flames and smoke rising into the air, when Ikram had looked back at frantic honking and seen a white cab speeding towards them. The sunrays reflected off its windshield had seemed to him the eyes of a beast, and a man's torso was visible hanging from the passenger side. Convinced they were about to either become the latest victims of the terrorists who were battling Airport Security Forces, the Rangers and the army commandos at the airport, or the latest victims of the city's perennial turf wars, in which various factions were trying to kill each other and all of them were trying to kill policemen, he had turned around and screamed in Billa's ear the one word guaranteed to provoke an immediate reaction.

'Bhagao!'

Take off.

Billa had gunned the engine without comment. Neither of them had any illusions about their chances in an ambush.

The old motorcycle had done its best, but even with its portly riders leaning forward, the cab had pulled abreast of them before they had gone a hundred yards. Ikram had only then thought to fumble for his holstered pistol, praying it would not jam again, praying his bladder would hold, praying he would at least get a posthumous medal for reluctant bravery, that his scanty pension would go seamlessly to his family, but the cab driver's shout had stayed his hand.

'Will you stop? I need your help!'

'You're saying that to trick us,' Billa had shouted back without slowing. 'We'll stop and you'll beat us to death while filming it on your cell phone!'

'My cell phone doesn't have video,' the driver shouted back, 'pull over!'

'You'll put it on YouTube!'

'YouTube is banned!'

'You'll use a proxy!'

'For god's sake, you gainday ka baccha, will you stop already!'

'No!'

'Stop or I'll ram you!'

Billa slowed down, grumbling, and risked a look to the side. The cab driver pointed to the man in the passenger seat, who was still leaning out of the window on the other side. 'You need to check this out!'

The constables pulled up to the side of the road. The cab pulled in ahead of them.

'What's the problem?' Billa felt more confident once the cabbie came around the back and shook hands with him. Ikram kept his hand on the holster of his pistol, partly to hide its age. The young guns were better equipped these days and he didn't want to look a fool.

The cab driver gestured to his passenger. 'You have to get him off my hands before he fouls up the inside of my cab anymore.'

The passenger vomited down the white door and hung, limply.

'Is he sick?'

'He's drunk.'

'Why didn't you just kick him out then?'

'And leave him to be run over?'

'Where did you pick him up in the first place?'

'At the airport. It was total chaos. Everybody was running here and there trying to jump on any transport out. He jumped into the cab before I could take a look at him, with a family. They made me drop them by the side of the road after a few minutes, the state he's in. I would have put him out then too but the Rangers started yelling at me to keep moving.'

'How do you know he's not a terrorist?'

'He's drunk! Terrorists don't drink!'

'How do you know? They do those drugs, don't they, that keep them going for days? Who's to say they don't drink too?'

'Why don't you take him in and find out if he's a terrorist?'

'Not our job. Terror suspects go straight to the Rangers today. Or the army. Take him back and hand him to them.'

'And if he's not a terrorist they'll keep him anyway. Or kill him or make him disappear. I'm not having that on my conscience. You want that on your conscience?'

The passenger moaned as the constables examined him more closely, taking care not to step in the puddle by the tyre. Ikram tried a commanding 'Oye! What's your name?' The man groaned. 'It looks like it's all out of him now. Why don't you just drop him to his destination?' Ikram said.

'He doesn't have a destination!'

'How could he not have a destination?'

'How the hell would I know!'

'Why didn't you ask him for a destination?'

'I did. He started crying!'

'Why didn't you ask him nicely?'

'I did ask him nicely. I don't know why he started crying.'

'This stinks,' Billa was grim. Tears meant loss. Loss meant trouble.

'You've got to get him out of my cab. Arrest him for drinking or something.'

'Fine,' Ikram took his hand away from his holster, 'but you'll have to drive him to the station, I'm not risking vomit on my uniform. It's my last one.'

At the station they'd cleaned the drunk as best they could, pouring a bucket of water over his head as he whimpered in the sunlight of the yard. The compound was empty, except for a few chickens scratching in the dirt, and the tea boy sitting on a stool in the kitchen listening to the radio. Everybody else was at the airport, even the intelligence officers. Then they shoved him into the holding cell. Still, the rest of the day's catch, a petty thief, two pickpockets, an old man who'd taken a wrench to his foreman at a garment factory, had retreated into the corners farthest from him. The water had washed the regurgitated chunks of airplane food from the front of his pink shirt, but some remained trapped in his beard. It was a half-hearted beard, five days growth under thick lips, bright eyes and a high forehead. He stood immobile in the spot he'd been shoved to, staring straight ahead, bug-eyed. Collared dress shirt, khaki slacks, polished shoes, a real leather engraved wallet. Quality. Probably quality enough to offer a significant bribe once he'd sobered up enough to offer one.

The constables and the cabbie had argued about the five hundred rupees they'd found in the wallet. There was a credit card, but that was of no immediate use. The cabbie claimed the cash as his fare, which would otherwise have to come to out of his own pocket, and payment for the boys who would wash his car. His poker-faced opponents had explained they were unable to bypass the procedures of arrest. The contents of the wallet were also in custody and could not be released till the investigation was over. The cabbie had left cursing, saying he was going to have to go back to the airport and double charge anybody left trying to flee and it would be all their fault.

'We can put that part in the report, say we resisted the cab driver's attempt to extort money from us,' Billa said as they finished a quick cigarette on the porch, resolutely ignoring the dull thuds in the distance.

'What's the point? It was only five hundred rupees. Four hundred, now.'

'Let's hope he doesn't remember exactly how much when he sobers up,' Billa gave Ikram a disapproving look.

Things were tight, these days, tighter than they'd ever been. The SHO, newly transferred from a post in interior Sindh, had the crazed sheen of the born-again law enforcer. He knew his underlings whispered it was the prosthetic legs caging him behind a desk that had gotten him such a plum posting, that he was just a morale-boosting mascot, and he had a lot to prove. Close as he was to retirement, Billa didn't want to lose his pension over a paltry sum.

'Relax. The state he's in, it's doubtful he'll even remember his own name unless we tell it to him.'

'I remembered it easily. Because it's your name.'

'What does Asfandyar mean, anyway?'

'How the hell would I know?'

'I think it's a Pathan name. There's that ANP leader called Asfandyar, isn't there?'

'You're not a Pathan. He doesn't seem like a Pathan.'

'He seems like a good kid.'

'You can be a Pathan and a good kid.'

'You're twisting my words.'

'I'm not. I'm just pointing out that someone else could twist your words.'

'I'll be quiet then.'

'I'll believe that when it happens.'

They stubbed out their cigarettes, both of them thinking that Asfandyar Ikram in the holding cell did indeed seem like a good kid.

They hadn't been as sympathetic to him the first half hour, standing on the other side of the bars trying to threaten some sense out of him. He had no luggage, no phone, just the wallet. Did he know anything about what was going on at the airport? What had he seen? What had happened? Who was he? Where was he from? Where had he gotten the alcohol? Did he know how much trouble he was in?

The two young pickpockets, teenage brothers, nabbed simultaneously after one had turned back to break his sibling free of a planned victim's angry grip at a weekly Meena Bazaar, had tried to help. One of them had pointed out to Asfandyar that the constables were talking to him. The other one had walked right up to him and gently turned him around so he was facing the bars and his interrogators, but the dazed man had just kept standing there.

'You think this is the old days, when the police picked you up for drunkenness and gave you a bed and a blanket and a cup of tea in the morning before sending you back to your wife? It isn't. Those days are gone. You're looking at a jail term. Worse. We'll send you to the Rangers and tell them you're a terrorist if you don't talk!' Billa had tried to frighten him.

The drunk had burst into tears, frightening Billa in turn. Billa was terrified of tears. He had seen too many. 'Hey relax, kid, it doesn't have to come to that. I was only joking about sending you back to your wife!'

Asfandyar had only sobbed harder.

'Every time you say wife he cries,' said the old man who had taken a wrench to his employer's head. 'I think what you have here is a marital dispute. I've seen it before, you know, we all have. The strongest of men crumbling, like mud cakes in the sun.'

'Who asked you, old-timer? Why don't you be quiet and let us do our job?' Ikram said.

'I was only trying to help,' the old man grumbled. 'What's going on out there anyway? What's happening? Where is everybody?'

'Like you tried to help your boss? Your kind of help we don't need,' Billa had composed himself and tried again. 'You, Asfandyar, stop crying!'

'The chutiya deserved it. Why should this one stop crying? Is crying a crime now?' The old man wouldn't give up.

'Not when I make it happen to you, which I will in a second if you don't shut up!' Billa wouldn't either. It was about face now. The constables had to win, or they'd lose control of everyone in the cell and the day would seem longer than it usually did. He cursed the overcrowding that meant only serious interrogations, of serious criminals, could take place in private.

'That's a threat, that is, I'm going to complain. I'm going to tell the media when they come to see me.'

'The media isn't going to come to see you, toothless, you only wounded your boss. Nobody died, nobody cares.'

'Well, I'll tell your boss!'

'Go ahead,' Ikram said. 'He'll be very angry indeed.

Angry that we swaddled you like an infant instead of suspending you upside down like the shit that you are.'

'I'd like to see you suspend me upside down. Actually, I'd like to see you try. You're both so fat you'd probably die of a heart attack if you lifted a bag of flour.'

Billa, who was sensitive about his weight, hit the bars of the holding cell with his baton. The old man's grumbles subsided. Asfandyar cried on.

'Asfandyar,' Ikram said, 'son, talk to us. Tell us what happened. Maybe we can work something out.' He wanted an easy afternoon, in which Asfandyar would make a confession, offer financial incentive for them to forget it, and they would negotiate. He wanted another hour in the safety of the station instead of the danger of the world outside it.

'Oh just talk to them, will you, or we'll have to listen to their whining voices all day long,' the old man said to Asfandyar. 'I'd rather listen to a bomb blast than to these two being efficient. Where did the bombs go off today, by the way? We all heard them.'

'I wonder how you'll sound when I pull your tongue out,' Ikram said.

'I'd still make more sense than you. What's going out on there? Come on, tell us.'

'I'm going to break every bone in your body if you don't shut up.' But Ikram said it without conviction, and after a few seconds of trying to stare each other down they both looked away. It was too early in the day and too pointless.

Everyone in the room, except possibly for the drunk, knew Billa and Ikram weren't the mean kind of cops. If they'd had what it took to choreograph encounters, inflict torture, kill with paperwork, they wouldn't still be constables. If they had what it took, they'd be out there with the others. 'Come on, Asfandyar Ikram, we already share a name, sort of, you might as well share your story with me too.'

'If I told you, you wouldn't believe me.' Asfandyar spoke softly. Everyone leaned forward in anticipation of his next words. 'You'd laugh at me and ask me to tell you another one.'

'I don't know about that, son,' Billa said. 'We've been policemen a long time. I doubt there's a story we haven't heard.'

'Yes,' Ikram said, settling next to him, 'if it's a story we haven't heard before we'll let you go, immediately.'

'We've got a few stories you've never heard, will you let us go too?' the younger pickpocket said.

'Wait your turn,' Ikram wagged a finger at him.

'But we were here first!'

'You're too poor to be worth a listen, you young fools,' the old man said. 'Chunnu-Munnu here are thinking with their stomachs.'

Billa banged his baton against the bars. 'Talk!' he commanded Asfandyar.

'What day is it?' Asfandyar rested his forehead against the bars.

'What's the matter with you? It's Sunday,' the young

pickpocket looked at him with contempt. 'How drunk do you have to be to forget what day it is?'

'I'm not drunk enough to forget. I wish I was. I was just asking to confirm it. That's one of the things I've learnt recently, confirm. You must confirm what your gut tells you.'

'When your gut is done telling you to confirm, can your mouth tell us more important things?' Ikram was keeping his hopes of a simple confession alive.

'The story began on a Sunday too. A Sunday some months ago. It was election time. No, it was right before.'

'We don't need to know your life story. We just need to know the bit that got you here,' Billa, unlike the SHO, hated detail. Detail, like tears, made life more complicated. Detail meant long sentences.

'It's part of how I got here. It's why I got here. Do you want to know or not? Be honest. I know how hard you people have to work in this city. What I saw earlier ... what you're up against ... I have the deepest admiration for you and I'm already ashamed to be wasting your time.'

'They're not up against anything. They're just jumped-up class monitors. Forget them. I want to know,' the old man said, 'I don't have anything to do till the media gets here.'

'If these honorable men here give me permission...' Ikram – after a few seconds searching, and failing to find, mockery in the tone – nodded.

'On that Sunday many months ago, I came to Karachi to bury a father I thought was already dead. My mother had led me to believe he was dead, when I was growing up in Lahore, but that morning she woke me up and told me he'd been alive, and now he was dead, and I had to go to Karachi to bury him. So, being the good son I was raised to be, respectful of my mother, obedient – you'd understand why if you met my mother, she is a remarkable human being, remarkable, she teaches and guides, oh what a disappointment I must be to her – I got on a plane and I came to this city for the first time.'

'That sounds quite believable till now,' the old man said, 'a funeral is the only reason people visit us these days.'

Billa banged his baton on the bars. He went to the wooden bench along the wall and sat down.

'When I landed, I was supposed to be picked up by my father's best friends. But there was nobody at the airport. I got a cab to the address my mother had given me, my father's address. Once I got there, a chowkidar gave me the keys and I let myself in. I found the three old men, uncles they said I should call them, and I found them drunk. They wouldn't tell me anything about my father, or what I had to do, till I agreed to have a drink with them. Now, I didn't drink, at that time.'

'Is that why you're making up for it now?' Ikram couldn't resist.

'I didn't drink, at that time, because I thought it was wrong. Not just wrong in the eyes of man, but wrong in the eyes of god. I used to think those things mattered, you see. My mother has always taught me they do.'

'Easy, son,' the old man cautioned Asfandyar, 'you don't want to say something you'll regret later.'

'I used to think those things mattered, and now I don't know if they matter is all I was going to say.'

'That's even more dangerous!' The old man chuckled. 'Walk around telling people you don't know how to think about something and they'll insist on telling you how to. You'll die of boredom.'

'That night, I drank a lot. I didn't even like the taste of it but I thought I had to, because I wanted to prove I was a man. Have you ever been around men like that, who make you feel like you're not a man unless you do what they do? I doubt it. You all seem a lot wiser than me. I've wondered since if my lack of backbone, my desire to fit in, came from being raised without a father, but I stop myself from thinking past it. I can't blame other people for who I am, can I? None of us can. Even now, saying it, I feel like a coward, hiding behind my mother. Forgive me for being weak and trying to. I know we all understand how important mothers are, and I'd hate for you to think I'm disrespecting them. Anyway, I drank and drank and drank, and they told me all about my father. He sounded like a man unlike men I had met before. I remember that part, then I don't remember after. I remember waking up the next morning and going to his funeral. I remember burying him in a navy cemetery – my father used to be in the merchant navy. Then I remember burying him again, at sea, from a wooden sailboat, with a beautiful woman on it.'

'Hang on, I thought you said you buried him in a naval cemetery?' Ikram said, proud of his alertness.

'I did. You're very quick. I see I can't put one over you. Turns out we buried someone else. A homeless man who died on a pavement whose body we bought from a shelter. I say we, but I wasn't party to it. I mean, I was, because I was there, but I didn't plan it. You don't have to believe me. I expect you won't. But on my mother's life I played no part in that.'

'I see.' The man was all over the place, Ikram thought, making no sense. And stupid too, to talk about stealing bodies and dumping bodies in a police station. He decided to let him keep talking. Sooner or later something would slip that the policemen could latch onto. 'So you stole a body and buried it in a graveyard and then buried the right body at sea on a boat with a beautiful woman on it.'

'Exactly. This beautiful woman, she was the daughter of one of the uncles. They told me she was the daughter of one of the uncles. She wasn't beautiful actually. Your women aren't. I'm sorry. I don't mean to say Karachi woman aren't as beautiful as Lahore women. I just meant to say that in Lahore our lives aren't so hard and all of us have more time to enjoy the little things, more time to take care of ourselves, so we have women who look so perfect you feel you're looking at a doll. I'm sure you have some in Karachi too. But I haven't ever been here long enough to see them. I've really only seen one. This one that I was telling you about. Sure she wasn't perfect-looking but this one, this one was alive.'

'What a pity. If she was dead you could have buried her in outer space.'

Asfandyar gave the old man a reproachful look.

'What! I'm just saying, so far you've buried one in the earth, one in the water, it's only logical to think the next one should be in space...'

'No. It's okay. I understand. I must sound like a madman and you're a good man to call me on it. When I say she was alive, I meant she didn't just sit there. She moved. She talked. She was friendly. It was an awful day and she made it better just by being around. She made everything better just by being around. Even those awful uncles, they were better when she was around. And she'd wait on them, she was considerate. She was kind. She was so kind that that night, after her father and the others left, she stayed behind to help me clear up my father's flat.'

'Why did your mother tell you your father was dead all those years if he wasn't?' Ikram said.

'That comes later. I'm trying to tell the story the way it happened. It's the only truth we have, chronology. Everything else is so fluid. We don't know why things happen, but we know what order they happen in. So, this girl, she stays behind to help me clear up the flat. Oh I forgot to tell you that I had been drinking all day.'

'You said you didn't drink then,' Ikram was still alert.

'I didn't. I thought it was just something I was doing for a day or so, while I was in the crazy city, because that is what the people I was with were doing and I wanted to fit in. So I drank and drank. And then when the others left the girl stayed and...'

'We know what happens next,' the old man chuckled. 'A man and a woman alone, the man drinking ... it's inevitable. We know what happens next.'

'I don't,' one of the young pickpockets said. 'I need details. I'm too young to know. You should educate me.'

'You're too young for this kind of education, friend. I know you're in jail but you still have your whole life ahead of you. You don't have to end up like me. And anyway, I don't remember. Well, I didn't remember till later,' Asfandyar said. 'When I woke up the next morning, she was gone. And then the uncles came to see me.'

'I don't like her father,' the old man said. 'He shouldn't have left her with you. What sort of father leaves his daughter with a drunken young man? Those uncles of yours, they aren't good people.'

'That comes later!' Asfandyar put a hand on the old man's wrist for a second, a light touch, as if to ask for reprieve because his train of thought was in danger of derailment. 'The uncles came to see me and I was so scared. I'd started remembering, you see, bits of the night before. Just little bits, about me and the woman, and it seemed like we had ... I'm so ashamed to say it because we're all god-fearing people here but it seemed like we had...'

'Inevitable. Didn't I say it?' The old man was smug, 'Inevitable.'

'But I wasn't sure,' Asfandyar continued, 'I wasn't sure. I knew only that even if I'd just imagined it, even if it was just the devil playing with me, I had to hide it, because her father would have killed me if he found out. He seemed like a very angry man when I'd met him, so I said someone had broken into the apartment and stolen all the money. And kidnapped her. I had to explain why she was missing, you see. Because they said she wasn't at her father's house.'

'Money?' Ikram sat up, 'What money? You didn't say anything about money.'

'Money? Did I say money? I meant the money there must have been in an apartment.'

'Was your father a rich man?' Billa asked.

'My father? No. No, he wasn't a rich man. I don't know why I said money. Like I said, I was panicking, so I thought I'd say there had been a robbery and that was why the woman was missing. They'd taken her for ransom. You have a lot of robberies here too, don't you? This is a hard city. A harsh city. I don't envy you your jobs. You have the hardest jobs in the world. I don't know how you do it. You have so many robberies. And so much death. And isn't there a lot of kidnapping too?'

'More than anywhere else,' Billa agreed, proudly.

'I tried saying that, that she'd been kidnapped, but they didn't believe me. They knew already, you see. That she had stayed over. But they didn't know what we had done. Or they said they didn't. They said she'd called them at night and told them I was fine but I kept drinking and then I found pictures of my mother and father together and I wasn't and then I suddenly attacked her and tried to kill her and she was injured and I was unconscious and could they come get her so they came and got her and took her to the hospital and she was there very badly injured but her father didn't know and if he knew he would kill me and she knew that so she'd told them not to tell him because I hadn't meant it, I was a good man who'd just had too much to drink and been overwhelmed by the anger I must have held in my soul all those years that the two people who were supposed to love me and protect me couldn't, but they knew and they would protect me if I'd only go away and never see her again so nobody would know except she would know and they would know and her father wouldn't know.'

'I've only been listening to you for a few minutes and already I don't know either!' Ikram was getting frustrated. Perhaps letting Asfandyar talk had been a bad idea. He was no closer to why he was drunk in a cell than before he'd started. 'Fast forward!'

'I'm sorry. I didn't mean to be incoherent. It's just, there is so much I want to say but I'm a simple man and I struggle to find the words to say it. Thank you for listening though. Just talking about it, I feel like a weight is lifting. Clarity embraces me. But the story ... so I did as they asked. I left. I got on a plane and I flew back to Lahore and I decided to get married.'

'One minute, one minute,' the old man stood up, 'you're telling us you got drunk and thought you had beaten a woman, or maybe done other things to her before beating her, and you ran away and decided to get married?'

'Yes.'

'Up until now I thought you were lying,' the old man clapped Asfandyar on the shoulder, 'but now I think you're telling the truth. Because that's the most logical thing you've said so far.'

'How is that logical?' the younger pickpocket felt cheated of more than detail. 'How do you go from beating one woman to marrying another?'

'You'll understand when you're older,' came the answer. 'When men hit women they're just expressing that they want to touch women. So his hitting a woman then getting married is actually quite intelligent.'

'I wish I'd had a father like you, or brothers,' Asfandyar said. 'I wish I had. I don't know if what you're saying is true but I know that it's helping. That's how we learn to think, isn't it? Listening to other people. If I'd had a brother or a father, maybe I'd have known how to do that. But I don't. I've never had that. Maybe I would have been a better man if I had. But I was talking about getting married. Except I didn't get married, I got engaged, and I wanted to get married immediately, and my mother and my fiancée seemed perfectly happy with it, but then the days turned into weeks and then into months. Every time I brought it up, they'd say there was still so much to do. I'd say I just wanted a nikaah and they'd get even angrier and accuse me of not knowing that things have to be done properly. I'd ask what could be more proper than a nikaah and they'd say it was my fiancée's big day and I was determined to ruin it for her. I didn't want to ruin it for her. I just wanted to get married. If I got married, I'd stop thinking about that other woman. I'd still be the man I was before I came to Karachi.'

'What was her name?' Billa asked, now caught up in the story, which in no way mirrored his own. 'What was the other woman's name?'

'Sir, it pains me to say this, but I can't tell you.'

'Why not?'

'Please understand that this is no way a reflection on you but I don't want to share her.'

'You just shared a lot of her! If she even exists.' Billa was hurt to not be trusted.

'If I don't name her, she'll just be a woman. If I name her, or describe her, you'll have a little of her too. I don't want that. She's evil. I won't let her pollute other people too. I won't let her pollute you.'

'One minute, one minute,' the old man waved his hand in the air, 'how did she get to be evil? You told us she took care of everyone, and then you possibly took advantage of her and beat her so hard you put her in the hospital, so how does that make her evil? Doesn't that make you evil?'

'I haven't told you what happens next. When I do, you'll understand. See, after I left and went to Lahore and those months of running back and forth in pursuit of some perfect wedding day that I had absolutely no interest in, I got to thinking about her all the time. Not my fiancée. This other woman. I'd be puttering along The Mall in the wake of my mother, going from one embroidery-wallah to another, one shoemaker to another, one tailor to another, and I'd see her. I'd see her everywhere. I'd see her in the shape of the dressmaker's dummy. I'd see her feet in the khussas in the store windows. I'd see her in the yellow of an egg yolk – she looked lovely in yellow you know – and I'd start thinking I was a monster. I'd taken that delicate, lovely creature, and what had I done to her? I wasn't a monster. I was worse than a monster. I was a dog. I was a demon. I began to hate myself. And the more I began to hate myself the more I wanted the marriage to happen already. My wife would make me better, I thought. Women make men better, don't they? Or at least they're supposed to? I'm rambling now. So finally a date was set.'

'Wait!' Ikram said. 'Were you drinking during this time?'

'No. Absolutely not. If my mother or my fiancée had caught me drinking I would have been in the hospital. I didn't touch a drop. I swear. I was sober. I was more than sober. I was depressed. But I kept on. I lived. I woke up, I breathed in and out, I went to work, I ate, I slept, I woke up, I did it again, thinking there was only so long I had to do it, then I would be married and I would no longer have to be the only person I had to live with.'

'What about your fiancée? Didn't she notice there was something wrong with you?'

'My fiancée always thought there was something wrong with me. That's why she wanted to marry me, I think, so she could fix me. What angels women are. Some women are. Mothers and fiancées and wives are. Are you all married? Yes? No? I wish you all every joy in the world.

You deserve it. I can tell just by looking at you that you deserve it. Anyway, so the date was set. It was the final week. Everyone was celebrating. Well, my mother and her family and my fiancée and her family were celebrating. I was celebrating too, smiling, hugging, but inside I was crying. I hid it because I didn't want to hurt anybody. I was paralyzed with fright that someone would say, 'No, wait, this man is a monster, he's a demon, he's a dog'. But it didn't happen. Only I knew. And it was killing me. I'd have nightmares about it. I'd have nightmares about her. They'd start out as dreams, beautiful dreams, with water and a woman in yellow, and they'd turn into nightmares with her body floating on the water, her fragile brown limbs broken, her perfect skin lacerated by my claws.'

'Is he just drunk or is he high on something?' Billa muttered to Ikram, but Ikram shushed him. He was rapt. Asfandyar's story was straight out of a Turkish soap opera.

'In the last week, my colleagues at work organized a get-together for me. It was just we men, you know, when a man marries his friends take him out, maybe organize a little something. But they didn't organize a little something for me. They knew I'm not that kind of person. At least, they thought I wasn't. We all did. The devil had done such a number on me that even I did. We had dinner in a nice restaurant. They paid. There was much ribbing, and dirty jokes, and as the evening went on, the conversation turned, as it inevitably does in these situations, to women. Women other than the fiancée of the man who is getting married, of course. We can't talk about her. Or about each other's wives. Or mothers. Everything else is fair game, isn't it?'

They all nodded.

'One of my colleagues was recently married too. In fact, he'd gotten married right after I'd come back from Karachi after those terrible two days. He'd gotten married the week after, and I'd missed his wedding because I was at home pretending to be sick but secretly shivering in disgust at what a lowly creature I was. He'd gotten married, and they'd arranged a night for him too. But it wasn't a night like that one, the clean one, for me, because he wasn't like me, you see. He was a normal man. He had normal interests. They'd had a little something. A little something so pleasurable, so diverse, so well-resourced they'd even flown in a girl from Karachi. The others wanted to see pictures. Even if they had been there. They wanted to remember this girl, to see this girl. So he showed them pictures on his cell phone. I didn't want to see them. I wasn't that type of man, you see. I was pretending to not be that type of man. But they insisted, said there was no sin in it. I decided to oblige, the food was making me sick, their laughter was making me nauseous, I was thinking about my fiancée and what I might do to her, what the demon in me might do to her, and I wanted to be distracted, the devil told me I had a right to be distracted, so I looked.'

Asfandyar took a deep breath and gripped the bars more tightly. His audience inhaled.

'It was her. The girl from Karachi, flown in the day after I'd gone back. It was my girl from Karachi. My uncle's daughter. Who'd spent the night. Who I'd put in the hospital with life-threatening injuries. Who I thought I'd put in the hospital with life-threatening injuries in a drunken rage. There she was, one day later, whole, unmarked, dancing, smiling, uninjured. She was a whore. She'd been a whore. I'd been had. The uncles had done a number on me. They'd used her to set me up so they could take the money.'

'What money? You said there was no money!' Ikram pounced.

'Did I? I must have forgotten. Thank you for reminding me. It's so difficult to think straight when you are under as much pressure as I am. I'm not making excuses though. I sound like I am, but I'm not. I'm trying not to. I'm doing the best I can. God, let it be enough. There was a little money. In the apartment. Which they took from me under the pretence of paying her hospital bill.'

'How much?'

'A lakh. Just over a lakh.'

'That's a very complicated scam to play for such a small amount.' Ikram was unconvinced.

'Maybe there were other things too, in the apartment, that I didn't know about that they couldn't take while I was there, like my father's wedding ring. I'd seen it in the picture of my parents together I found before I got upset, you know. It was a thick one, solid gold. Oh those poor people! Nobody gets married thinking they'll create a child to torment with absences and silences,' Asfandyar said, before nodding gratefully at the old man, who was gently squeezing his shoulder in commiseration. 'The point is, I was taken by a whore. And like a chump I had no idea. Till the night before my wedding.'

'What did you do?' The young pickpockets were sitting with their arms looped together.

'I got up and I walked out of the restaurant. I had an awful thirst but I had no idea where to slake it. I walked and walked. I walked for hours. I walked to mochi gali.'

'Didn't anybody come after you? Didn't anyone call you?'

'I sold my phone to the first man who came up to me. He gave me very little for it, but it was enough to convince another man to find me a room and something for my thirst. People say there is evil abroad everywhere these days but I tell you there is still good. We're a good people. We take care of each other. We help each other. For a trifle we let others cross our threshold and offer our hospitality. Why we are so misunderstood, I don't know. Why things like what is happening outside happens, I don't know. I see you agree with me. May our true colours be revealed in all their glory one day soon. Inshallah. So I drank and drank. It was morning. I was supposed to be at my own nikaah. I drank some more. I fell asleep. I woke up. I drank again. Then I went to the airport and used my credit card to buy a ticket and came to Karachi. I came out of the plane and the airport exploded. Not the whole thing, bits of it. Everybody panicked. Allah stepped on our anthill. The ants scattered. I don't remember getting into a cab but I did. And now I'm here. And I'm still demon and monster and dog. I always have been. But now I know which woman I have been that for.'

'Why did you come to Karachi?' Ikram asked, sensing the man had more to say.

'I've finally figured it out, you see. All this time, I've been kicking myself, hating myself, even hating those uncles for making me drink. If I hadn't had a drink, none of it would have happened. Then, after I saw her picture, I realized it was all the whore's fault. She was the devil's agent. She played me. She played me for a fool. Now I'm not a weak man. I'm a bad man, or I've done bad things, but I'm not a weak man. I can fix this. I will fix this. I just need to balance this out, find the balance, make it right. The one thing I did before I walked out of that restaurant, I took the number of the pimp who'd flown her to Lahore from my colleague, and I saved it.'

'I thought you sold your phone?'

'I saved it in my heart. I'm good with numbers. It's what I do for a living. What I did for a living before this happened. Now my mother might not even have me to support her when she's old. She might die destitute and homeless.'

'What are you going to do?'

'What am I going to do? First, I have to get out of here. If you'll let me. Then, I'm going to call that number, and talk to the pimp, and get that whore's address. When I think about all the people I've hurt. My mother, my fiancée … it's the only way to make it right. You have to take evil, and you have to rip it out by the roots. And once you do, you take those roots that you've ripped out, and you hold them up, to the sight of God, and when He sees them, then and only then does He forgive. So I'm going to go to that whore. I'm going to find her. And I'm going to kill her. '

In the afternoon rays from the window set high in the wall behind him, Asfandyar glowed gently, as if he, and not the sun, was the source of the light.

The tea boy – a child with a face so innocent even the SHO hadn't had the heart to lock him up for the crime he'd committed but instead given him a job – barreled through the door yelling, 'Do you know how many of those bastards we've killed so far?'

'Fuck off little insect,' Ikram kept his eyes on Asfandyar.

Silence flowed from the men in the cell and the men in the corridor onto the boy. He retreated. Ikram on the bench felt a chill travel up his spine and shuddered. 'That's not a bad story,' he said. 'That's not a bad story at all.'

'Revenge,' the younger pickpocket breathed.

'Revenge,' his brother agreed.

The old man and Billa had nothing to add, but nodded. Sense, a through line, had been found and declared true. That was when the petty thief, a man in his forties who till then had been curled up on the wooden bunk with a blanket over his face, so still they had forgotten he was there, spoke.

'Fools,' he said, 'this isn't a story about revenge. This is a story about love.'

# SEVEN

THEY HAD LOVE ALL wrong, he said. It wasn't a thing of flowers and film songs but knives and bullets. In the old days men had had it right, but in the now, a steady drizzle of hard women's soft words had obscured the truth of their own hearts. Asfandyar had said he wanted to kill the whore. He had said he wanted to do violence to her. What was violence but love? Did everybody understand?

'I understand that you're crazy,' the old man said.

The toothless one had gone soft, the petty thief said. He'd had the makings of a real man once. Perhaps he still did, otherwise he wouldn't be in a cell for letting his limbs do the talking, but he'd gone soft. Five minutes ago he'd told Asfandyar he understood how he could go from beating one woman to marrying another, and here he was pretending he didn't understand the dark places love lived. Love lived in caves of pain and teeth. They had only to think of how they had all been born.

Nobody spoke.

And he meant love, he clarified, not lust. They had lust all wrong too. It wasn't a thing of knives and bullets but zips and buttons. Lust never said it wanted to kill somebody. Love did. Lust passed. Love didn't. Lust forgot. Love didn't. This poor young man, the petty thief said, for months walking around thinking he wanted to break a body in anger. He did want to break a body, he had memories of breaking a body, but men and drink had wrapped them in lies and fog and all he could remember and obsess about replicating was the breaking.

'It doesn't matter why or how he wants to break a body,' Ikram said, 'what matters is that he wants to break it. We can't let him go around breaking bodies.'

'He didn't say he wanted to love her,' the younger pickpocket pointed out, 'he said he wanted to kill her.'

Asfandyar wasn't talking about a permanent breaking, the thief said. He was talking about the temporary breaking after which the parts reassembled themselves with kind spirit. The kind spirit of the kind of breaking that was so rare people no longer knew it if they saw it. The constables and the toothless one were fools, he went on, walking the world with their eyeballs in their palms. The two pickpockets could be forgiven for their youth, but the older men? They hadn't just forgotten the faces of their fathers, they had forgotten the faces of their lovers. Here was a young man still courageous enough to let his heart guide him, even if he didn't know it either, risking planes and taxis and the wrath of mothers and fiancées, and what were they doing to help him? They were wasting the momentum of Asfandyar's flight, caging it under the flimsiest of pretexts, instead of setting him free and letting it carry him to its ecstatic denouement. That was the world they were supporting, if they had the balls to face it, letting those who would dismember hold sway on their streets, and those who would knit together die a thousand little deaths in captivity. He would spit in their tea if he could, but it would be a waste of his saliva.

Billa hopped from the bench and banged his baton on the bars, repeatedly, till the petty thief lay back down and covered his face with his blanket again. The constable was furious. He felt violated without knowing why. By accusing him of being an enemy of love, the thief had stolen a dignity of self-image Billa had not known he still had.

'I know all about love,' Billa yelled at the man in repose, 'I've been married for twenty years!'

'Nobody said anything about marriage,' came the muffled reply. 'What does marriage have to do with love anyway?'

'That's what I say to my wife when she complains I don't love her,' the old man had picked a side, finally. 'She never used to say such silly things before I got her a television. Worst decision of my life, getting her a television.'

'Television isn't the worst though.' Emboldened by the sudden support, the thief cast his blanket off and sat back up. 'The worst is those digests women read. With the poetry-spouting heroes who are always sweet and docile. As if that's what we are. Real men, and you have to be a real man to feel love, real men aren't predictable and obedient, real men aren't sweet and docile. Are we, old-timer?'

'If I was sweet and docile, I wouldn't have brained my boss with a wrench now, would I?'

'I liked a girl once,' the older pickpocket volunteered. 'I used to follow her home from school every day like a dog. She didn't give me the time of day. I saw her last year after I dropped out of school and I ran past her and stood in front of her blocking her way. She had to walk around me. I did that every day for a whole week. The last time she slipped me a note with a cell number on it. I spoke to her every night for a while, till her parents found out.'

'What happened?' Billa was discovering he was interested in details after all, just not the sort of details he was used to.

'They moved away. I haven't seen her since.'

'Didn't you call her and try to find her?'

'He did,' the younger brother spoke for his suddenly morose sibling. 'First her father answered and said if he called again, he would kill him. Then the next time, the phone was off. He tries every week still. We keep telling him to forget it but he won't. Sometimes he just sits there and whimpers.'

'That's love, like I told you,' the thief said, 'invisible knives and silent bullets.'

'Look, hero, this nonsense has gone on long enough,' Ikram stood up and tried to take charge of the conversation. 'Asfandyar here has wasted everyone's time with…'

'Love isn't a waste of time!' the older pickpocket shouted. 'This is why everyone hates the police, you know! You're cold bastards! You'd rather arrest couples than criminals. You think love is terrorism!'

'She loved him too!' His sibling lined up behind him. 'Don't call her a waste of time!'

'Have you all gone mad? I'm not calling her anything,' Ikram said, 'I'm just saying I don't know ...' He meant to go on and say he didn't know how a search for facts had turned into a minefield of emotion, with men exploding at every step, but the old man chimed in.

'Of course, you don't, you heartless brute, how can you when you're an unfeeling machine!'

'Is that what your wife says to you in bed?' Ikram regretted saying it as soon as he had said it, by which time it was already too late. The old man sprang from his perch on the edge of the bunk and, grabbing the bars to hold himself steady, unleashed a torrent of abuse followed by a recital, at high volume, of a ghazal castigating the harshness of the world to the eyes and hair and lips of lovers. Ikram, the old man paused mid-torrent to declare, should listen carefully because he was that harshness made form and flesh. To put on the uniform, he said with contempt, he had stripped off his humanity.

Beside him, the older pickpocket began screaming the lyrics to an Atif Aslam pop song about learning to live with the daily accrual of loss. His younger brother followed his lead with an off-key rendition of the theme song of the drama serial *Humsafar*, in which light and shade shifted places but lovers remained steadfast. From the bed, the petty thief struck up a bass raga leading into Mehdi Hasan's classic rendition of how, if they separated now, those possessed by passion would meet only in dreams.

From the corridor came the sound of running footsteps and the tea boy burst in to tell Billa and Ikram they were being summoned to explain the ruckus.

'You little snitch ...' Billa took a step towards him.

'Go fuck your own mother, no I didn't!' He disappeared around a corner before either of them could grab him.

The lyrics and couplets rose in volume to pursue them down the corridor so that by the time they reached the SHO's office and went in, they had to shut the door after them to block it out. Still, the wood too sang with the strain of keeping the ruckus out. When the SHO asked for an explanation, Billa had to shout, 'It was the drunk who started it,' twice before he was heard.

That is what Billa and Ikram were both considering as they came in after their cigarette break and started down the corridor to the cramped room they were expected to do the paperwork in. Neither spoke. Neither knew what to say. The trajectory of the story was out of their pay grade. They knew only that they didn't know what about it was true and what about it was not. They knew only that they both felt shell-shocked.

They sat across from each other at an old wooden desk, scored so from countless nibs it looked like a back, flogged, from the days when drunkenness could lead to that. It was Billa's turn to write, so he pulled the thick register in which they composed the First Information Reports towards him and picked up a pencil. Later, corrections and revisions made, he would go over the pencil with ink. He put it down before he could even write the date.

'I love my wife,' he said.

'Of course you love your wife,' Ikram replied.

'I love her and she loves me and we would do anything for each other,' Billa continued. 'I love her and I've never wanted to hurt her.'

Ikram nodded. He sensed he did not need to say much, just listen.

'She's given me four children and peace at home. But if she disappeared tomorrow and I didn't see her a few months, I don't know if I'd give everything up and go off in search of her, just like that. That asshole of a thief is right. Did you see the way Asfandyar was crying? We've seen some bad men in here. He's not one of them. He's gentle. He's a gentle man. He doesn't want to hurt the woman. He just wants to see her again and he took off at the first inkling that he could. I love my wife. But I don't know if I'd do that for her.'

'She's not his wife,' Ikram said, 'she's a whore. And he's an innocent.'

'I'm just saying, don't we have bigger fish to fry, these days?'

'I suppose we do.'

With that, he too stepped into the path of the story Asfandyar had told them, and let it roll over him without resistance. Peer pressure might have done it. Or the rhythmic, peculiar nature of the words flung at them by the chorus in the cell. It could have been tiredness too, the tiredness of the same story day after day defeated by the novelty of this one. Whatever the reason, he stepped into the story his colleague and friend had already embraced, and did not demur when Billa suggested they scrap the idea of an FIR, and, for a change, help a man instead of simply stopping him in his tracks.

And that was why, a couple of hours later, a freshly showered Asfandyar Ikram, the front of his shirt still damp from the tea boy's wringing out, found himself standing across from SHO Moin agreeing that his incarceration was the result of an awful case of food poisoning brought on by airline food, and an exploitative cab driver, and a chaotic situation, and promising to call the cab company and complain as soon as he bought a new cell phone, like the helpful, efficient, kind constables Billa and Ikram were suggesting he do.

SHO Moin was suspicious, as he was of everything, but a few months in the city had taught him to pick his fights. This one, he sensed, as he wished the polite young man godspeed, wasn't meant to be his. Besides, when the dust cleared down the road and they began bringing the usual suspects in, they would eat this one alive. He didn't want that on his conscience either.

# EIGHT

ASFANDYAR STOOD OUTSIDE ALINA'S compound like a penitent, not knowing what terrible purpose he carried but not unfeeling of it. The morning's haze was beginning to clear from his mind and the bubble that came after it was pushing outward from his body. Clarity crept around him, revealing a destination found. A narrow, dust-coloured block of flats with a high black gate and a chowkidar outside. Defence View, the sign pronounced. Though all the view offered was a dual carriageway clotted with buses and a flyover carrying sedans high above.

The roads surrounding the airport had by then been clogged with Karachiites rushing to the spectacle as it wound up, but Billa and Ikram had walked him to a taxi stand a mile away and put him in an old yellow-and-black one after giving directions and money to the driver. Pimps didn't provide girls without references, they'd said, and he would never have found the whore on his own. They'd used the station line to call around and make a booking in the SHO's name. The first few calls had yielded no results. Nobody had heard of the girl. Then they had called a new entrepreneur in the market. He had professed similar amnesia, till Ikram had mentioned the prosthetic legs. He had heard of the new SHO already and was fond enough of his own appendages to be amenable to threats. Still, he had said, he wouldn't have passed on what he knew unless the girl's own pimp hadn't recently left the field.

'Don't insult us,' Billa had waved Asfandyar off when he'd tried to stammer his gratitude, 'what is a couple of hundred rupees and a phone call between friends?'

And they had parted friends. Even the dour one, Ikram, had grunted a goodbye after saying, 'A man has to do what a man has to do.' It was an incongruous image, but he had begun to see their city as a western, so when they ambled away, faint sombreros wavered over their bald heads and the thickened waists wore gun belts. The taxi was a horse. The men in the station that day might have seen it differently, but he knew he was a cowboy, riding for revenge, like in the black-and-white films he had seen on PTV as a child.

The way the story had galloped away from him and ridden over the men around him had taken him by surprise. What was to him a clumsy, error-ridden attempt to manipulate his way out of a jail cell by inspiring pity had turned into the opportunity he had set out from Lahore seeking being handed to him. He had never meant to tell them he would kill her, but it had flown out of his mouth and, miracle of miracles, not landed him in deeper water. Used as these people were to violence, perhaps they had developed immunity to the mention of it, took it as metaphor, until it became literal. Perhaps he had been channelling the spirit of Anis Nabi. The patriarch, he remembered the uncles saying when so many had shown up for his funeral, had always exerted a strange power over his fellow men. And his son now knew that the most crucial inhibition drink took away was the flexing of it. *But I'm not complaining,* Asfandyar thought. *If the spirit of that bastard has brought me here, maybe his spirit should take responsibility for what I am about to do too. Let his be the eyes that fall on her with revulsion. Let his be the hands that squeeze the life from her throat. And when they put me back in jail, maybe this time I'll end up with other monsters instead of deluded sops so desperate for love they'll see it in anything, even blood and bones.*

In some part of his consciousness, Lalarukh and Jehanara shrieked behind their walls. More bricks and mortar, they were silenced, and he walked to the chowkidar and asked for Alina Bibi's flat.

Finding out that was her real name had been a shock. He had been expecting a revelation of embarrassing commonness; she was a Shagufta maybe, or a Saima. She was, as it turned out, a Nur for her clients, and Alina for her friends. *How frequently the uncles must have used her to attain that exalted status. Friends to a whore. Brothers to a wife-beater. Robbers of graves and corpses. The earth should open and swallow them. It already has. This is hell. They don't even recognize demons. Shut up, shut up!*

The stairway was dark and clean. No paan stains in the corners, and on the landing before her flat a small potted plant on a red platter. She was house-proud. *A clean house is the only thing she can have to be proud of.*

He laughed out loud at the 'Mashallah' sign on the wall over her door and had to lean against the wall to steady himself. He hadn't eaten since the plane and lost most of that to projectile vomiting. The 'Mashallah' brought an image of his mother mouthing it when Lalarukh had walked into the room at their engagement, the tight beaded bodice lifting her breasts and pointing them in his direction, his sorrow that they no longer gave him an erection turning into over-compensatory groping in the two minutes the affianced couple had had alone before an aunt had swooped down on them together in the kitchen and shooed him out. He realized he hadn't rung the bell yet. He realized he was still a little drunk. The mosaic tile under his feet turned into the black-and-white tiles of his father's bathroom that he had showered in after his one night with her. *I had a night with a whore and I didn't even know it. If I'd known what might have I done to her? This is why we keep women in the home. Let the bitches out and see what havoc they wreak.*

He pushed away from the wall, tried and failed to smooth his wrinkled shirt, and rang the bell. He kept his arms loose and his hands relaxed by his side, his face impassive, so that should she look at him through the peephole first before opening the door – *whores must do that* – she wouldn't feel threatened. She'd open it. He'd look at her. He'd see the panic in her eyes, the knowledge that death had come for her because she'd messed with the wrong man, he'd take a step forward, she'd take a step back, but she was smaller than him and he was stronger still for his hate, and a minute later it would all be over.

*You haven't thought about what you'll do after that,*

*have you. Shut up. Maybe she'll fight back. Maybe she'll kick you in the nuts and claw your eyes out. I won't let her. What if she won't let you? Shut up. I'm just saying maybe you're not being entirely rational right now. I'm being rational. She ruined my life. She has to pay. Did she ruin your life? Or did you? Shut up, shut up!*

He rang the bell again and kept his finger on the switch for an extra two seconds. He heard movement inside, small feet – *she had small feet with pretty nails and the smoothest skin, she stroked the insides of my thighs with them* – and a distant 'Kaun?'

He didn't answer. She was cautious. *Whores must be in their homes. Let her come and see 'who'*. He rang the bell again. *She'll have to answer or the downstairs neighbour will come out and that won't be good for her, to let her neighbours see her clients. The cop who called her pimp said that, didn't he, that she lives a quiet life and her pimp was concerned that he was bringing filth to her instead of her to filth. What a good-hearted man he must be, to be concerned for his business interest. Well, he cracked, and filth is here. Filth is standing outside her door. And when she opens it and looks at Filth she'll be terrified because she'll know Filth is going to suffocate her. Filth will recognize filth. Filth will be a mirror. Maybe Filth will rape her first.*

The door flew open. A small boy looked up at him, bright dark eyes under a thick silky fringe. He yelled, 'Ami, it's some uncle!'

Alina came to stand behind the boy, put her hands

on the skinny shoulders. She was wearing a red and white shirt and white lowers. She was thinner than he remembered her. *All that dancing must take it off. Her breasts are smaller than they used to be. It's the shirt.* 'It's not some uncle,' she said, smiling so brightly at the visitor it seemed the sun had snuck into her face and bisected it, 'it's Asfandyar Uncle.'

'Can he come inside?'

'He can.'

The boy took Asfandyar's hand and pulled him in. And hearing the door close behind him, the click as the lock shut, the patriarch's son, limp without anger, heard it as the sound of a trap closing.

# NINE

WAS IT LOVE, THAT possessor of invisible knives and bullets, that slid silently, sinuously up Asfandyar Ikram's fingers and toes, over his limbs and into his mouth as he stared at the woman still smiling at him so that, when he opened his mouth to speak, he had no words to push past it and could only stare at her, mute? The boy, excited, tugged the visitor forward by the hand till he was standing in front of a plush foam sofa, then shoved him gently till he sank back into it. Across from him, on the wall, a picture of the Qabaa winked at him.

'What will you drink, Asfandyar uncle?'

*Oh my god! He's only a little boy!*

'Tea? Coffee? Lemonade? Water? I know where Ami hides the coke too!'

'Water, please,' Asfandyar heard himself say. *Why is he so excited? Does he know me? Has she talked about me?* The boy scampered towards the kitchen visible through an archway by the front door. *He's probably that way with all the uncles because they bring him presents to keep him occupied while they take his mother to the other room.*

'I told him about you,' Alina said, sitting down next to him. 'I told him I met a man who fell asleep on a boat. He was very impressed. I took him on a boat once and he had motion sickness. He wanted to know everything about the strange person who could fall asleep on a boat. I told him you might secretly be Superman.'

'I wasn't asleep. I was pretending.' *We were both pretending. Weren't we?*

'How are you?' She was still smiling. He noticed that she hadn't stopped smiling since she'd seen him. He realized that from the day after Anis died, he actually had no memory or image of her not smiling. She was one of those women who looked like they were smiling all the time, even when their mouths were asleep. *But she didn't look like she was smiling when she was straddling me. That made her serious. I made her serious. Of course you did, she's a whore and fucking is serious business.*

'How am I.' *That is not an unusual question. In fact, it is a normal question. It is the question people ask each other, friends and family ask each other, when they have not met for a while. For a day, maybe. Or a few months. What's a few months between friends and family? What am I to you that you would ask me that question? Who are you to me that I want to answer it?* 'I'm fine.'

'How are you?' he continued.

'I have no complaints.' The boy came in with a glass of water on a small tray and held it out to Asfandyar. He took a sip and watched Alina ruffle her son's hair, proudly, then nod towards the glass coffee table in front of them so he put the tray down on it. 'His vacations have started so we've been spending a lot of time playing Ludo.'

'I'd rather watch cartoons but mom won't let me watch TV anymore.'

'I'm sure you're a very good Ludo player,' Asfandyar said to the boy. *Children like praise, so you are praising a child. Because that is what you do, out of courtesy, because we are all courteous human beings and this is a perfectly normal conversation.* He snorted. Water went down the wrong pipe in his throat. He coughed and choked. 'I'm okay, I'm okay!' He waved the boy's small hands poised to pat him on the back away.

'Asfandyar Uncle, do you want to play Ludo?

'Uncle is tired, why don't you go play downstairs and I'll play with you later?' She took the boy's hand and led him to the shoe rack and clucked over him while he changed from slippers to sneakers.

*What a well-behaved boy. Every other kid I know would throw a tantrum and refuse to go. Nobody brings their kids up properly anymore. If I'd argued with my mother like Lalarukh's little brother argues with his, she'd have given me a tight slap. But she would have to train him, wouldn't she? Does he listen at the door?* Her white churidar pajamas gathered around her slim ankles. Her red and white cotton kurta was cut like a man's. *That's why her breasts seem smaller*. He could see her flesh-coloured bra under it, the curve of her stomach when she turned against the light. The boy turned around and around again till she reached behind the rack and pulled a cricket bat out and handed it to him.

*Anticipating need. That is the other thing about her. She knows who needs what, when. Conversation. Rest. Space. Touch.*

The door closed behind Alina's son. She leaned against it and looked at Asfandyar, who had put his glass down on the table and was staring at her. She wasn't smiling. He couldn't tell what she was thinking. She must have trained herself to be that way too, to hide what she was thinking or feeling. *She feels nothing*. He held her eyes till she looked down. *It's too late to be shy, Madam, but how skilled you are at pretending to be.*

'You look hungry.' She pushed away from the door. 'Can I warm some food for you?'

Asfandyar didn't answer.

'We can talk while you eat, or after. If you've come to talk.'

It was his turn to look down.

'Have you been here all along?'

'I flew in this morning.'

'The world is on fire. I'm glad you're safe.'

*My mother would have said my poor poor baby and smothered me.*

'Are you okay with home-cooked food?' she continued, 'I can order something else for you if you aren't. It might take a little longer than usual today but it'll get to us eventually.'

There was a picture on the wall by the kitchen, an enlarged passport photograph of the boy when he was a baby. Apple cheeks, a surprised look.

'Home-cooked food it is,' she decided. A lock of hair had broken free of the clasp holding it at the nape of her neck. She reached behind and tugged it. *She's nervous.*

'You don't have to talk to me if you don't want to. Will you just nod if you're okay with my cooking? I don't like to waste food.'

He nodded.

He followed her into the kitchen after a minute. It was larger than it looked from the living room. There was a table big enough for two against one wall, and the sink and cabinets in an L shape around the others. He sat on the chair she pulled out for him, put his elbows on the table by the plate she set and watched her as she took containers out of the fridge and stuck them into the microwave one by one.

She put serving spoons in the containers and gazed studiously at a calendar while he served himself. Then she sat across from him, not looking at his plate, or his face, as he ate. Neither of them said a word. When he finished the glass of water by his plate of daal chawal and achaar, she rose to refill it. After she'd put it back on the table by his elbow she stood by him for a minute. He didn't look up. She bent and kissed the top of his head then, tentatively. He looked up at her then. She retreated to her own side of the table. His mind was still. There were no thoughts. There was no second-guessing. He'd never felt as rooted in a moment as he was in that one.

'Teabag tea okay?'

He nodded again.

She washed the dishes while the water boiled on the stove. Water splashed the sleeves and front of her kurta. He traced the straightness of her spine through the translucent fabric, the way her hair caught the light and played with it, the way she hummed along to the music wafting from another flat through the kitchen window. When she raised a hand to wipe her brow, she left suds on it. When she turned to smile at him, bubbles and all, he smiled back. It felt natural.

'I never felt guilty about the money,' she said. 'Anis would have wanted us to have it. He had class, you know. He wasn't like the others. The one I was with before him ... anyway. I met Anis through him so I shouldn't wish him ill. I asked him once, when he first suggested working together, you're decent, you're educated, you've seen the world, why would a man like you want to be in the business? He laughed and said it was because he had seen the world that he knew we were all in the business, so he was only sorry that he'd had to grow old to realize we shouldn't feel any shame in admitting it to ourselves.' She took the cloth hanging on the oven handle and wiped her forehead. 'He always said I was his best girl. Towards the end I was his only girl. And he knew he had a responsibility to...'

Centuries ago, a mystic had compared holding on to anger to chaining a mad dog in a house. Sooner or later, it would break free to savage its inhabitants. It was the 'us' that unchained Asfandyar's. Links snapped, then came together in a different formation. The uncles, the impunity afforded by patronage, the money, the woman, the child. They hadn't done it for themselves. They'd done it for his father's whore. His pimp of a father's whore. And his pimp of a father's other son.

He was at the sink behind her. He had no memory of rising from the table to get there. His hand was on her throat from behind, the other on her shoulder, pulling her around. He didn't have any memory of telling them to either. But his hands had a life of their own, like his limbs had when he'd been in bed with her. She was fully turned, facing him, the small of her back pressing into the marble slab holding the sink. Her own hands rose, wet, delicate, panicked birds in sudden flight off the water, to grip his wrists. The imbalance she savoured in intimacy worked against her. She tried to say something. He choked her so the sound died. They stared into each other's eyes.

He had so much to say to her. He remembered the outpouring in the jail cell, the way the words had sprung from him without control, one after another, gushing. He thought suddenly of his mother. He began to wonder how much she knew, if she had been ... he choked harder. 'You whore,' he hissed into her face.

Alina dropped her arms. Her spine relaxed. She pressed against him instead of trying to pull away. Her pupils widened, offering nothing to read. Red tendrils raced from their corners to the irises. He knew that was his hands' work. She moved her hips. He realized he was hard and that his hands were loosening around her throat. Her mouth opened slightly. He stopped applying pressure but his fingers remained at her throat. *The thief was right!* He wanted to kill her in the way that really hurt. They remained locked in that tableau of terrible violence only the broken can choreograph memorably.

That was what the boy saw when he let himself into the flat to get his cricket ball, quietly, knowing he wasn't supposed to disturb his mother when she was with an uncle. That was why he raced to the nightstand for the gun he knew she kept there and why he stood in the doorway holding it up in both hands, his small sleek body trembling as he clicked the safety off.

Alina was attuned to the thinnest sounds. She heard it before Asfandyar, snapping forward so suddenly her forehead smashed into his chin. He would carry the bruise for days. She brought her arms up to part his and shoved him behind her as her child pulled the trigger.

'Ami?' There was faint embarrassment in the boy's voice, as if he wasn't sure whether he'd done something wrong or right. His arms wilted.

# TEN

HE LOVED TO CLIMB. On the tree in the courtyard and the worn climbing frame stripped of paint by small hands, he had no equal. *Speedy*, the others would call him when he was inevitably the first to the top of the bars in a race. *Hero*, a girl had said when he'd retrieved for her a kite that had come drifting to them from the city beyond the walls and come to rest on the topmost branch. Racing up the trunk he had ignored the twigs of the denuded limbs and on the ground the scratch map on his bare arms and legs. The flattery did not make him loquacious, it made him even more reserved, so the kids who sought to befriend him learnt the best way to do so was to leave him alone. Then he might come sit by them at lunch, or share with them, silently, a chocolate he had been gifted by the guard at the gate. The guard was a taciturn man. Nobody knew why he had taken a shine to the boy. The boy never spoke of it, or of anything, voluntarily, except for the gibberish he would utter when he had nightmares like the one he was having that time.

'My mother was a teacher,' the boy insisted. Matron's podgy hands pressed him back down onto the bed in the dormitory as she nodded, cursing the child for pulling her out of a deep sleep again.

'Of course she was, little one,' she said, secretly wanting

to slap him into unconsciousness but determined to keep her voice calm. The director had gotten very angry when she'd shouted at her charges last week. One more violation of the code of conduct and she would be fired, he'd told her.

'She was.' He stopped struggling and lay back down. She sat by him for two minutes in the gloom till he turned on his side and closed his eyes. He was an odd one, this boy. He must have been eight or nine, but he'd play around the other children in the compound instead of with them, like a toddler, as if convinced he wasn't really there. That didn't endear him to them either. Several times she had had to break up fights he'd gotten into because in the child world to be aloof meant you thought you were better than the others. The others would bring you down sooner or later. Once he'd had a hairline fracture. 'I fell on the stairs,' he had told the director sullenly when asked to name his bullies. The director had let it go, and told everyone to keep an eye on him. Donors weren't as accepting of accidents as they once used to be. There was only so much news carrion to go around. The vultures with cameras were always sniffing for stories.

'Why didn't you tell her what your mother taught, whiney baby?' Sibilant whispers came at the boy out of the dark after Matron had gone back to her own quarters in the centre. He had been weak and confided in an older boy in the first week. He had never made that mistake again. He curled the pillow up over his ears to shut the whispers out. *She taught men how to love*, he thought.

*That's what she told me.* The whispers kept coming till he fell asleep. If they penetrated his dreams he didn't notice because they weren't the worst things in them.

'If we call the police, they'll take you away and put you in jail,' Asfandyar Uncle had told him after he'd shot his mother. 'You don't want to go to jail, do you?'

The boy didn't want to go to jail. One of his other uncles was a policeman and he had told the boy about what sort of men ended up in jail.

'I don't want you to go to jail either.'

Asfandyar Uncle was a kind man to say that. The boy knew he'd done something bad, he'd done something awful. He'd understood, from the way the man had cried over his mother's body before pulling himself together and talking to the boy that he hadn't been trying to hurt his mother after all. He'd been trying to love her. She'd been teaching him.

'We have to go now. We have to leave, right now,' Asfandyar Uncle had said. 'Do you know where Alina, where your mother, kept her money and jewellery?'

He had shown him where. Asfandyar Uncle had pocketed it and helped him pack a small bag of clothes. He'd told him to put his cricket ball in it too.

'You never know when you might need it.' The man had tried to smile, but the boy felt he was looking at a skeleton. He'd taken the ball out of the bag, when Asfandyar Uncle was examining the jewellery closely. He didn't deserve to play anymore.

They'd walked all the way down the street to catch a rickshaw. The boy had said they could get one closer to the apartment but Asfandyar Uncle had shushed him and hurried him on. The first rickshaw driver had argued with uncle for a long time before speeding away. He'd tried two more before a driver said he knew where they wanted to go.

At their first stop, Asfandyar Uncle had told him to stay in the rickshaw while he hopped out and talked to a man standing before a high, gray gate. The man had shaken his head, stroked his beard and spread his palms before uncle. He'd come back to the rickshaw cursing and told the driver another address.

At the second, the police had closed the road and ambulances raced past the barricades. TV crews were massed there, waiting to be let in. There was a pall of smoke hanging over everything and the driver would go no further. 'There'll be another one!' he insisted. 'Trust me there is always another one!'

*This is hell, this is hell*, Asfandyar Uncle had muttered to himself for the next five minutes, till the boy had put a hand on his knee and squeezed. It wasn't hell. It was Karachi. Everyone knew that.

At the third stop, Asfandyar Uncle had spent a longer time talking to the man at the gate. Money had changed hands. His mother's money, he knew, emerging from the pocket it had been slipped into. He used to sneak into her stash and count it himself, when she wasn't home. There was an awful lot of it. Enough to buy every toy he'd ever wished for, every snack he'd been forbidden. He began to wonder if he should have told Asfandyar Uncle where it was. He wished he'd brought his cricket ball, after all. She wouldn't have minded. She had always forgiven him.

'Here we are,' Asfandyar Uncle had taken the boy's bag out and was pulling at his hand, like the boy had pulled at his hand when he'd entered their flat. Had that happened earlier that day? It seemed a long time ago. 'Come on.' The rickshaw driver, Asfandyar Uncle was indicating, should wait for him.

At the gate, he handed the bag to the guard, who put his hand on the boy's shoulder and began to push him in.

'What about my mother!' he had shouted as the guard's grip had tightened at his resistance.

He'd had to strain to hear the man's reply over the sound of the rickshaw engine sputtering as it pulled away. 'They're all dead,' Asfandyar Uncle had shouted. 'We're all orphans now! We'll have to be our own mothers and fathers!'

# EPILOGUE

# PAKISTAN STANDARD

YOUR RIGHT TO KNOW

Established Daily • August 10, 2013 • Shawwal 03, 1434 AH

## Metropolis Crimewatch

*City Reporter*

KARACHI: Eight people, including a woman, were killed in different areas of the city on Friday.

Three youngsters were found dead with bullet wounds in the bushes off Superhighway. The victims' hands and legs were tied with ropes and the bodies bore marks of torture as well as one bullet each in the heads. The identities of the victims have not been ascertained yet. Police said they were shifted to the Eidhi morgue after post mortem. They suspect the victims were killed and thrown and they are examining the area for clues. A case has not been registered till the filing of this report.

In a separate incident, a bus conductor was shot dead near his house in Pehlawan Goth within the limits of Gulistan-e-Jauhar police station. Billo, 31, son of Najib, was walking home when armed men opened fire on him, resultantly he received one bullet in his chest and died on the spot. Duty officer Khurram Shakil said the police believed personal enmity might be the motive behind the incident. The body was handed over to the family. No case was registered.

In yet another incident, a father and son were shot dead outside their house in North Karachi in the limits of the Khawaja Ajmair Nagri police station. The victims, Irfan and Imtisal 'Lucky' Latif, were sitting with their friends drinking tea when two men on motorcycles opened fire on them. The motorcyclists sped away. The son, 28, died on the spot. The father, 50, succumbed to his injuries in the hospital. Both bodies were released to heirs after medico-legal formalities. Police suspect personal enmity behind the killing. No case has been registered.

A case was registered in Surjani Town police station against unknown men for the killing of Rehman Gul, 28, who was shot dead on Street 9 of Yousuf Goth, by armed men. SHO M. Rahim said the victim was well known in the area and had no affiliation with any political or religious party.

Meanwhile the body of a woman was found from her residence in Defence View apartments, after neighbours reported a suspicious smell. The victim was known to her neighbours as Alina Bibi. She had received one bullet wound to the heart. The body was shifted to the hospital for medico-legal formalities. ASI Muzammil Rao said state of residence indicated a robbery. When this reporter asked whether there was any sign of the child the neighbours had reported lived with her, ASI Rao said these things could happen in custody disputes. No case was registered till the filing of this report.

## ABOUT THE AUTHOR

Shandana Minhas's first novel *Tunnel Vision* was shortlisted for the Commonwealth Writers' Prize in 2008. *Survival Tips for Lunatics*, her book for children, won the Karachi Literature Festival Fiction Prize in 2015. She also writes for stage and screen.